Behind Closed Doors

Trapped within traditions- No alternative whatsoever

by
Amita Tak

AuthorHouse™ UK Ltd.
500 Avebury Boulevard
Central Milton Keynes, MK9 2BE
www.authorhouse.co.uk
Phone: 08001974150

© 2007 Amita Tak. All rights reserved.

No part of this book may be reproduced, stored in a retrieval system, or transmitted by any means without the written permission of the author.

First published by AuthorHouse 6/29/2007

ISBN: 978-1-4343-1263-1 (sc)

Printed in the United States of America
Bloomington, Indiana

This book is printed on acid-free paper.

Acknowledgements

I would like to give a huge thank you to those who know me and are apart of my life as it is them who gave me the courage and determination to reach my goal especially my parents and family in which I couldn't do this without them. I do have many close friends who are a vital part of my heart and will remain to be. Since my childhood Rachael and Iysha who are my very close friends have provided me with so much support during my life I therefore bestow my sole gratitude upon them and maintain utmost credit for their moral considerations during the process of my book. Moreover, during the preparation and publication of my book I was provided with appreciation and continuous fortitude at my current job. I work with the most loving and caring colleagues that I greatly admire and will always remember them when confronting every event in my life. Therefore, Behind Close Doors is a bequest from me to them for their immense encouragement and time.

Preface

To the reader the story I am going to tell you is fictional. I hope you appreciate and enjoy the thrilling actions and events that take place in the story. Behind Close Doors is a novel I have always desired to write and today my ambition has been fulfilled. This is most likely my only book I will ever write, so please take care of this book as my full potential is embedded within this novel. Throughout the book there are many morals that emerge many of which are my sole beliefs in life. So please do consider them at your own will as perhaps many of you will interpret them with a complete different opinion to which I will not hesitate to comprehend. Further, since I don't state the beliefs in the novel the following paragraph illustrates the frequent use of my ethos in the novel.

The central character in the book who's name is Annika, is brought up in a very much old fashioned approach however, her brother and sisters bearing in mind are nurtured the same way don't take their father's traditional upbringing seriously. For example she doesn't socialise at bars and clubs. Annika believes this is wrong and causes corruption to one's behaviour; hence she doesn't drink alcohol or smoke this is because it means that she has to go against her father's faith. Secondly, she always abided to her parent's customs and never disrespected them for her own desires even if it means to give up her own happiness. Thirdly, never forget gaining your own autonomy doesn't mean to go against your parent's it means to stand on your own two feet as your parents won't be holding your hands for the rest of your life.

As a whole for those who portray life to be uncertain, the publication of my book depicts that dreams do come true and you can experience them if you maintain self-assurance.

Thank you for your time and comprehension for reading Behind Close Doors.

Chapter 1

It was a bright day in December year 2005 in the city of wondrous Wullington. This was highly unanticipated as you would have expected obscurity. The snow glistened with shine in December's breeze, the world imagined to be like it was embedded in a graveyard with absolute futility, silence was the essence of time, the clouds trailed slowly and Annika knew it would be a very long day. She felt as if the day was going to be endless and the outside creation shouted to her of an unforeseen event, however she only feared this slightly.

Annika knew she would have to take the step of telling her father the truth about her older sister, she was full of light and enthusiasm but the revelation of her sister's secret to her dad was going to be a long process, which would involve tears. When it came to the thought of it her throat became tight and she struggled to catch a breath, then the vein in her forehead came to the surface of her skin and revealed the pain and distress within her fragile body.

It was early evening the clock had shortly ticked to five o'clock she had just got back from school and was sitting on the floor in her bedroom thinking about what would happen when her dad came from work. Usually Annika's father comes from work about half past five but surprisingly he had come from work approximately 15 minutes early. As he entered through the door it was like a gust of wind had embossed the house transforming it to an antique looking house. Annika heard his large footsteps come up the stairs and in her room she was walking back and forth at the same time biting her nails which were near non existent. If you would have seen Annika at this moment of time you would have thought she had seen a ghost or something because nothing could stop her body from trembling. As he had made his way up to his bedroom the girl next door kept imagining what tomorrow would be like, she kept herself busy to speed up time, nevertheless it seemed that time was working against her, she wasn't quite up to speed, in other words was rusty.

Annika kept talking to herself,

"What would he say? What's going to happen?"

She muttered these questions constantly, what was it that hideously frightened Annika? She thought back to the days when her dad tried to commit suicide and how he used to hit her mother, whom was very young back in the days. Coming back to the present there were faint sounds coming from outside and she could hear a dog's bark in the distance, somewhat trying to caveat something. Annika peeped through the curtain and at the window all she could see was sleeted roof tops and a clear white sky. It was more like a painted picture. Thereafter she opened her door slightly with the sound of a creak making her jump a little and she walked out of her room towards her father's bedroom. For a moment she stood still and then timidly and in a reserved manner she knocked on her father's bedroom door. "Come in" he moaned.

Chapter 2

Annika's father's name was Tony Manda he was a common sort of man in his late 40's nearly hitting the half a century mark in about 2 months time, he had a beer belly and a croaked voice. It tells on a man when they smoke, but he always felt in himself that he was young at heart being the youngest in his side of the family. As Annika walked in, Tony looked directly at her whilst he was opening the post; she was white as a piece of cloth thinking that her dad knew what she had to say.

"What's the problem?" he shouted, swallowing her saliva her mouth opened but she could barely talk, she thought she had gone deaf for a minute. All of a sudden it was like she came back to reality and a loud voice from within her shouted, "Sheena's got a boyfriend." Tony got up, his temper raging with pure anger in an instance walking towards Annika and asked her to repeat what she had just said.

"Dad, you heard me the first time, it's the truth. Sheena's got a boyfriend" he then slapped Annika across her face. The news had inflamed his temper causing Annika to cry and shout "it's the truth I saw her with my own eyes" she then ran out of Tony's room and locked herself in her own bedroom, double checking the door was locked with insane fear of what would happen next. She spread across her bed and looked directly up at her God's picture that hung right above her.

"I've told him now, I can't turn back the clock, I'm scared and I don't want to live anymore- there's no point, I don't have a reason for living God; I've betrayed my own flesh and blood, I don't deserve the right to go on. What is the point of living in this family if we can't have our own freedom? God you wanted your children to be happy so why can't Sheena be happy, let Ashley be part of her life and he will treat her like she's the most beautiful, most kind, most generous person in the world, showering her with love and gifts like she deserves. He'd want her to settle down and have his children and they'd have the perfect family. They have loved each other for so long now, so why should they be denied of such happiness for their own future? God I thought that couples were made together in heaven and marriages took place on earth, so why are you breaking every possibility of them ever being together?" Annika continuously hollered at her God in anger but also in tears which resembled scars on her porcelain skin. She was a beautiful angel and everyone knew exactly what her objectives were in life; to please her father. She was too kind, loyal and selfless making her unique in every way. The tears kept coming and she sank her face in her soft pink blanket leaving a light indentation from her face, yet drowning the blanket with her sorrowful tears; she kept her face covered on her blanket for such a long time causing her to fall asleep for about half an hour.

Chapter 3

After half an hour Annika had woke up and she heard a very big sound, it sounded like someone was smashing plates. She felt frightened like a stray alley cat scurrying away from a mongrel and begun to think that this was all of her fault. There was a feeling of a volcano about to erupt in Annika's room but all of a sudden Annika started to cry and her voice was full of so much pain, she screamed and walked unexpectedly to her chest of drawers and took out a pair of scissors. With the scissors she was about to slash her own wrists however downstairs her mother called her whom had arrived from work

"Annika get downstairs now!" and relentlessly she dropped the scissors, unlocked her room and came running down the stairs into the lounge. Rita i.e. Annika's mum commenced and shouted at Annika saying "What have you done? Why did you tell your father?" She remained silent and had no answers to any of her mother's questions. It was obvious Rita already knew about Sheena but she stopped herself from telling Tony. This was because she knew he would act in such a harrowing way and let loose the inner beast, which she had so timidly over the years locked away. Her marriage to Tony for 30 years was full of commotion, crying and havoc it was like living in hell. As a result Rita started to suffer from high blood pressure and "dry eye" this was where there was barely any moisture left in your eyes, hence Rita had cried for the past 30 years of her life. As the children grew older they prevented their father from hurting their mother.

In the lounge everything was absolutely shattered to pieces even the ceramic ornaments bought from India on previous occasions. This once, beautiful house turned into a house, full of horrors. Annika sitting in the lounge feared her father's reactions. Tony was sitting on the floor holding his head in his hands, he was growling like a famished wolf that had not eaten for weeks. He grabbed hold of Annika's hair and told her to ring Sheena at work. Annika looked in the diary and dialled Sheena's work number, Sheena picked up and Annika spoke with a nervous tone of voice with her words barely making sense. Sheena spoke back saying "have you told dad yet?" Annika exploded with a cry and Sheena knew straight away that their mission was successful. Tony then grabbed the handset out of Annika's hand and he threatened Sheena, he spoke with such a evil tone of voice "if you don't get home within 20 minutes, you will see my dead body" he smacked the phone down into its receiver causing a plastic piece to fall off. Tony cursed at Annika, but Rita comforted her and said "don't worry everything will be sorted, lets just pray to God and hope for the best." Annika sat down on their comfy green sofa and her face was pale with her tears resembling Niagara Falls. In great confidence she held onto her God's pendant around her neck and worshipped and praised God in some way to get gratification throughout the rest of the evening hoping for good luck. She had faith.

Chapter 4

The skies began to darken like the skies of Annika's future, all Annika wondered about was the terrible mission Sheena and she had planned. She wished she could turn back time and stop herself from telling her father the truth about Sheena.

As the evening closed Sheena walked through the door, Annika was frozen with fear and she wished that Sheena didn't even come home at all, as she prophesised the night was going to be very extensive.

Yesterday night was a moment to remember for Annika as she couldn't stop thinking about what Sheena had told her to do "you've got to do it for me Annika, otherwise I will never tell him about me and Ashley. We have been very close for over the past years, do you remember when you were about 12 years old and you used to go against me well everyone did, mum,

Adi and Kareena. I felt so lonely and isolated from this family, however I knew that dad still had trust within me and he used to say Sheena would never do that if someone commented something bad about me and he was assured that I would be the successful one." Annika sat there thinking, the idea emerged in her head that perhaps what Sheena had just told her could have been akin to emotional sympathy for her as she replayed how her life was when she was young. Hence, Sheena had pre planned to disclose her relationship with Ashley to Tony in which she was depending on Annika to do. The reason for this was because Sheena knew how close Tony was to Annika and that he would always listen to Annika and nobody else. Therefore, you can postulate how Tony felt towards his youngest daughter where he had maintained an imperative trust. Knowing Tony was a harsh and strict father was it possible for Annika to do what Sheena asked her to do? And would this be acceptable for Tony? As a whole it was much of a struggle for Annika now.

From the night Annika accepted to tell Tony about Sheena's boyfriend she couldn't sleep at all on the same night. There were sounds of sirens coming from the distance, ever since Annika was a child whenever she heard or seen an ambulance she would pray for the patient inside to get better, but all she forgot to do was care for herself. The symptoms of neurosis began to appear upon Annika at the age of 17 that night; she constantly kept wide awake because of the thought of telling her father about Sheena disturbed her with anxiety.

To understand Annika as a person you had to adapt to the fact that she prayed every night to her God, she would speak like God was nearby and he would always be listening to her prayers. When it came to describing her connection with God in words it was very difficult. Unfortunately, tonight she didn't have that sense of feeling because whenever a situation confronted Annika her sole belief was down to destiny and destiny was controlled and planned only by God. Her eagerness expressed the notion of blame upon God.

"Why did you bring me to this turning point, now I am stuck in the middle, I can't take sides, there is no such thing as taking sides in families. I am the youngest in this family and tonight I feel like the oldest purely because I understand both sides."

On every occasion when there was a crisis in the Manda family, Tony would make Annika feel guilty and make her choose between him and the rest of her family. It was dependant on Annika's decision, if she had made the wrong decision Tony would sway the blame upon Annika and thereafter she would run to her God and ask why?

Once Sheena had entered through the front door Tony thundered straight towards the hallway and dragged Sheena into the lounge like she was a helpless puppy and all Annika could do was watch feebly. Tony shouted all the odds at Sheena

"What the bloody hell were you thinking of doing? One day I'll just leave without telling my idiot parents, is that what you think of us? That we are stupid and we wouldn't find out about your dirty little secret, we weren't born yesterday" Tony blasted at Sheena.

"It's not a dirty little secret, I am bloody 25 years old and you still treat me like I am a child I can make my own decisions now. I don't need you or mum because you have treated me like shit since I was young so why do you care about my relationship. I bet you are glad that I have a boyfriend?" with no regrets, Tony slapped Sheena across her face, leaving a red mark against her fair skinned face. "So you think you will get away with it now, well madam you've got it totally wrong" Tony yelled.

Annika looked at her dad and all she could see was rage in his eyes, he was boiling with fury and his eyes were blood red. Tony grabbed Sheena by her hair and keeping hold of her hair in his hands and was practically pulling it so that she couldn't free herself. Tony saw this as a punishment for her mistake. With utmost strength Annika got up and held her dad's arm so that she could pull it away from Sheena's hair but it seemed like Annika was causing more pain. In great sudden he pushed Annika away and threatened Annika and also

Rita not to come near. Tony then blasted at Annika "you flipping idiot I know you, you little smarty pants trying to take your sisters side, well it isn't working now is it?" Annika got up with full determination and she bit hard onto Tony's hand virtually causing his hand to let go of Sheena's once silky hair.

Chapter 5

Someone had come in from the front door, until the person came into the lounge they didn't know who to expect. It was obvious it was someone from the Manda family as they all had the key to the house. Kareena had just come back from work and she walked directly into the lounge without any expectation to what was on the other side of the lounge door. She had worked as an I.T trainee for a small established firm in the middle of Tilton; the company was called *'Techno Fab'* presumably *fab* meant fabulous. Kareena was the oldest daughter of the family however she was very reserved and vulnerable, you could say she had a wild side to her only when you got to know her deep down inside. Annika was ecstatic to see her "I'm glad you are here" she expressed. Kareena walked up to Tony puzzled "what's going on dad?" she said in confusion.

He replies back in complete anger quoting "why don't you ask your sweet little sister?" Kareena looks down to Sheena who is crying in vain "Sheena what's up and why is there so much mess?" her delicate voice replies "he knows about Ashley" "WHAT! I mean who the heck is Ashley?" acting very surprisingly.

"Come on Kareena you know what she is on about, don't act all innocent" Annika shouts across the lounge.

"Well, well you all bloody knew and kept the old man in the dark, don't say you didn't Rita your in the act as well?"

Tony walks up to Rita whom walks backwards bumping into the wall "DO I HECK" Rita exults.

It was striking half past ten in the night, Tony walked around the lounge with great ambivalence, he was shocked and didn't no what to say or do but he was defiantly assured that Sheena could never meet Ashley again. Tony was completely authoritative over his family and too self disciplined, so the decision he would make would be bounded and something what his family would not go against. This was because in the past he would have always decided what was best for his family without consulting his family. The rest of the Manda family were reduced to agreeing with him and nobody dissented.

On the contrary there was one time when Adi rebelled his judgment this was about six months ago when he went out with his mates without telling Tony, he came back around half twelve midnight, when Adi walked into the house it felt like he had collided in to a brick wall because he was slapped across the face by Tony. Tony was all fired up that not even the North Pole could cool him down. There on Adi didn't go out till late and if he did he made sure he was back by ten to be on the safe side, or in other words to obey his father's orders and rules.

It was little things like these that made the Manda family go against Tony, you couldn't blame them it was the 21st century a time of liberty and democracy. Despite all this Tony was still living back in time and someone had to change him and bring him forward to this day and age. This was definitely a difficult challenge to undertake and maybe it was Annika's task to change her father from a control freak to an understanding father.

Coming back into the present Annika watched her dad think hard and straight it was an ugly sight because she didn't know what was cooking under his restrictive mind. Annika thought about earlier on when she had the strangest illusion of this day to be never ending. She considered that it was noticeably her fault because if she hadn't agreed to Sheena's plans then she wouldn't be in such a tangle today. Knowing that her father would act in such a daunting manner she still decided to go ahead with it, this was the worst case scenario imagined, what was the alternative? Nothing was the answer to this question because nothing could change Tony. Tony kept hurting Sheena he wanted her to suffer because Tony had always drilled in to his children's mind that they could never have a relationship with someone before marriage, they could never drink or smoke and could never go to bars and clubs as it would lead them astray. These so called pleasures for a teenage of the 20th century were forbidden. Tony would hit his children to justify his action no matter if they were a girl and 27 years old when you consider Kareena's age. In Freudian terminology he would have explained Tony's behaviour as using one of his defence mechanisms which was called rationalisation.

Annika's father was the youngest in his family therefore, perhaps he would have been the less controlling one however, he was the opposite bearing in mind told his children that he had seen the nightlife when he was young himself and that he experienced having girlfriends before he got married to Rita. So why did he erase this right to learn for themselves from his children? The reason being was that it was horrible and not good to experience thus this was why he was over protective of his children not wanting them to see what he did.

Annika had got up and went straight into the kitchen she rang Adi off her mobile to tell him to come home immediately. When he picked up the phone she cried down the phone to him and a few words were exchanged. Adi was 19 years old he used to be such a sensible boy but when he hit 18 he went completely haywire. Annika described him to be a victim of this socialising society whom manipulated you to go against your family values that had been taught to you. However, it was possible that because Tony was very strict on him being the only son in the family, Tony still didn't give him the freedom he wanted. Hence, Adi perceived this to be unfair also that he became jealous of his mates as they boasted that their fathers had made a lot of money for them kept for the future. But Tony didn't have one possession under his name therefore Adi saw his tomorrow to be bleak.

In Asian culture families, boys were distinguished to be the man of the family and girls were remarked as a burden because they cost more to be wed and don't have any further use as they can't carry on the family name; which was of great importance to a traditional restrictive, controlling father but that was the old generation principle maybe Tony ruled his life against these old traditions but he was assured that Adi wouldn't get a penny not until he matured himself.

Chapter 6

The streets were empty; everyone was asleep in their comfy beds. But in the Manda family the night was to be eternal. Adi walked into the house about half an hour later after Annika's phone call. He had been working since he was 16 as he knew that he had to stand on his own two feet and that one day he would have to pick up responsibilities of looking after himself and most likely a family consoling a wife and preferably two children. Annika's face shone when she saw Adi, he dropped his bag on the floor as he entered the lounge because it was totally annihilated. "What the bloody heck happened in here?" Everyone was silent

"will someone explain to me what is going on?" Annika got up and walked towards Adi and she spoke reluctantly, uttering

"Sheena has a boyfriend called Ashley she has been with him for a very long time" she had stopped there because Adi had put his hand in front her mouth because he was astounded to hear Annika saying this in front of Tony. In bewilderment Adi went up to Sheena

"Why do you have to do this, forget about this Ashley guy, there is no point because there isn't no hope in this relationship"

"Why should I sacrifice my happiness for a father like this? Just because he is worried about what everyone else thinks, how dare he, allow his children to be kept under lock and key, just for his own benefit, to keep his so called spotless name clean? Why can't we be happy like all those kids out there? I want to have a lovely and pleasant life with someone who I love" Sheena in turn spoke back.

"LOVE, what do you mean love, you know you aren't supposed to love someone until after your marriage" Tony shouted. He grabbed Sheena by the arm and dragged her across the distinctively cold, tiled floors to the front door. Annika and Adi tried stopping Tony from doing something morally disturbing.

"Look can't you see what you are doing to this family, you are ripping us apart" Adi began to say to Sheena,

"We were never a family in the first place so why do you maintain this belief, just because you can't get your own way. I don't care I am following my heart even if it means leaving this family at least I still have my dignity" Sheena feebly gets up and goes straight upstairs to her bedroom locking herself in there "where the hell do you think you are going?" Tony shouts but Sheena purposely ignores Tony. Inside her room she starts to pack her bags and then after 20 minutes she comes out of her room all ready to go, but surprisingly Tony stops her from going and he locks the front door.

"You are going no where. I have decided that you can't see your boyfriend anymore and that's final"

"You can't stop me" Sheena replies

"You wanna bet, now get back upstairs with your bags and when you come back down bring your car keys and mobile phone" he slowly says careful not to make a mistake.

From there on Sheena knew she was stranded and goes back upstairs with her luggage and later comes back down with her possessions that were demanded off her.

Chapter 7

It was 5th December the Christmas month, it was after 12 o'clock in the night, and everyone was sitting in the once beautiful lounge. After ten minutes silence Tony had got up and said to Sheena "Tomorrow I am going to your part-time job to tell them that you are quitting your job, no ifs or buts. It's final." Sheena couldn't say or do nothing, Tony had planned to keep her secluded until the day she regretted what she had said and done. Sadly, for Annika she had to stop her work experience at Sheena's full time job, she did a placement every Wednesdays in the finance department, Tony turned around to Annika and explained to her that she had to quit her work experience as he didn't want Sheena or Annika to mix in, he knew that Sheena would corrupt her the wrong values, Annika was speechless after that.

Tony didn't at all understand his children's happiness and ambitions all he cared about was taking control and showing the outside world how respectable and customised his family was yet behind close doors it was terribly different. After an atrocious evening the Manda's decided to go to sleep.

The next morning, the tea was bubbling on the gas, it was a freezing Friday morning and the birds were cheering at 8 o'clock. Annika poured the milk into the tea and left it on full gas, she was shattered from last night and a cup of tea was a short term solution to her problems. She then dazed into what happened last night and the shocking news of her to stop her work experience made her more than vacillate, because she was only 17 her work experience was very vital to her life, it was a step up the career ladder to the real business world. For her age she was doing really well, as she also worked part time on the weekend, Annika's occupation was a catering assistant for a restaurant; she had been working since she was 16. Unluckily, she had to give up her work experience all because of Sheena but the sole person to blame was her dad because he had finalised this. Tony, only thought of the best for Annika, and if he trusted her so much he should have had faith in her that she was too sensible to even have a boyfriend if that was what he was afraid of.

Annika, constantly thought about the unique morals in life that existed, this was what made her inimitable and caused her friends and relatives to praise her, her thinking was often based on a much higher level and visceral explanation. Her auntie once described her as "such a caring and selfless character with everyone's best interest at heart."

Consequently, she kept asking herself questions or she would refer to God, "why does my life get affected? Losing my work experience meant a lot to me, I do everything right, I don't go out, I do not certainly drink I cook everyone's food, I clean the house, attends to everyone's needs before and the list just goes on but it all came down to one thing and that was to lose my dedicated responsibility because Sheena has a boyfriend. Can someone please explain to me what have I done incorrect in my life?" Why did Annika think drinking alcohol and going out was bad? These products and facilities were made to be used and it was part of socialising, how was it possible that it made people ill-mannered they weren't abusing the facilities and substances?

There was complete silence in the kitchen, then suddenly a spilling swish sound takes place, it was the tea it was overflowing the saucepan, in an instance Annika turned the gas down and poured the hot piping tea into a long green thermos. The thermos was for Tony's lunch for work, usually Rita would make it but she was still asleep since last night's never ending incident. Tony came down the stairs; he put on his shoes and walked straight out of the front door to his car, leaving his lunch behind. There was nothing surprising about this because every time there was a crisis in the family Tony would be in a bad mood causing him to leave his lunch behind as usual, therefore you would always know when Tony was in an appalling mood. He'd certainly loose his appetite, yet with her magnificent training, Annika would still manage to make her fathers lunch.

The Friday had passed on by, virtually like everyone was lifeless, in the Manda house it was definitely freaky Friday. Sheena had rang in sick at her full- time job this was because she was in so much pain that she had to go into A&E, when she got there by taxi as she couldn't afford to drive, she had to wait for two full hours until it was her turn to go in to see the doctor. After being called in she had to go and have an x-ray done, the doctor had told her that she couldn't even drive for 2 weeks and that she would have to take time off from work so that she can fully recover. Tony had pulled on Sheena's hair very tightly causing to sprain the back of her neck all the way down to the bottom of her spine. Sheena cursed at Tony every single moment of that day and she had told herself that she will never forgive Tony for the rest of her life.

Ashley kept ringing Sheena but Tony had taken away Sheena's mobile therefore he had no way of contacting Sheena. The only way he could contact

Sheena was through Annika. On that same day he rang up Annika but Annika didn't even pick up the phone. This was because she was very frightened to speak to him. Having the thought at the back of her mind that Tony would find out about this and he would then never forgive her. Ashley must have suspected by now that the mission Annika and Sheena had planned was successful and if she answered his calls, what would she say to him without even breaking down to tears first? Annika decided that she wouldn't receive any calls off Ashley but a few moments later he sent her a text message saying

"Please ring me back if not, answer my calls what has happened to Sheena? Was your plan successful?"

Following the message Annika decided to miss call Ashley and within a few seconds he rang her back. She answered his call and with great confidence she explained to Ashley what had happened last night, at the end of the call Ashley began to cry,

"Thank you for being there for Sheena and me. What would we have done without you, whatever happened last night was not your fault it was written in our destiny, but God will sort everything out" he said to Annika

Additionally, Annika knew that agreeing with Sheena was perceived as a right decision by strangers, what could she summarise after what Ashley had told her? Was she right or not in her way of thinking? There were a numerable amount of questions that gathered in Annika's mind.

Chapter 8

Due to the cold weather everyone had the sniffles besides Annika. She always kept herself strong but it was an awkward explanation when it came to Annika having the cold. She would always have the cold after the winter season which was mainly in the summer season. It was a chilly Saturday and Annika was at work, it was always the busiest day of the week especially when it was near the Christmas period, there were up to at least 200 customers that came to the restaurant, hence a mountain pile of dishes stacked up, the seating area of the restaurant was always full with customers, bags of food needed placing and the hot food was constantly on the go every 5 minutes and money was rolling in the till, it was definitely a job to remember for Annika.

The weekends would go by for Annika as most of her days were taken up by school and then attending her job. She made great friends at work but Annika was such a shy girl, compared to her work colleagues who were the complete opposite. Perhaps this was due to Tony, as he was so restrictive to his children, hammering at them that they can't go out to enjoy themselves as it changes your behaviour to become negative. Not only that, he stopped Annika from cutting her hair, going to concerts when her favourite band came, or even shopping with her mates, Tony was excessively protective. Once again Annika explained this in Freudian terms as he was her favourite psychologist, he would have evoked the theory of a parent and child relationship, meaning that if the parent didn't nurture the child lovingly and securely then the child would become neglectful when they are a adult but in Annika's case she was too intelligent to even think of disrespecting her parents. Or another explanation was using developmental psychology this was based on the level of parenting styles, in Tony's case he would have been theorised as an authoritarian parent, the child in theory isn't capable of succeeding individually in the future.

Unbelievably Annika disagreed with this vindication because it was putting the sole blame on the parents which was wrong. Annika was definitely triumphing academically as her major priority was to never lose hope in education and as it was the best option to pursuing the wonders of life. Taking into consideration that her family and religion were of equal importance however, Annika knew that her parents weren't always going to be there for her, this was why she wanted to learn how to become self-determined as it was for her far less reluctant to stay attached to her parents for the rest of her life.

You might be thinking up until now that the Manda family's future forebodes bleakness and when will light be shed upon the family, if you just keep the aspiration that a lot of Annika's good deeds will definitely pay off for a more fortunate future then you are positively on the right track. In some circumstances because Adi isn't much of a sport and he doesn't act like an ideal 19 year old he doesn't put in any effort into working hard; as he currently left his job at royal mail and from there on he only ever sits at home wasting away a fully functioning body and the opportunities that might face him in the outside world. Furthermore he had applied to university but he does not attend any of his lectures, surprisingly they haven't excluded him from the university because of his attendance record. Adi had become completely defiant of Tony's regulations this was why he stayed over the night at his mates or even girlfriends place without notify either Rita or Tony. It was Rita though who worried about him frequently because it was her maternal love that caused her tension for her one and only son. Adi often promised Rita he would one day become a rich man and he would take his mother out of this place to a place in which she deserved. He was almost like her saviour, the one and only person, simply because of his gender, who could save her from a bed that she had, herself made, but did not want to lay in.

On the other hand his relationship with Tony was akin to enmity, Adi ignored whatever Tony said to him and he would regularly shout at Tony portraying that because Tony hadn't made much wealth and inheritance for him he would mouth off expressing that he will just have to do it himself and become affluent one day. As Adi was maturing, Tony was ageing therefore he became helpless at times, Annika was afraid medically something would happen to Tony and in Annika's eyes Adi was to blame, promising that she would never forgive him. Nonetheless, even though Tony wasn't exactly open-minded and comprehensive he still nurtured his children to be mentally and physically healthy, so she couldn't even if she wanted to, go against Tony.

In the evenings, the fire place would be on full blast and the warmth from the heat comforted Annika, she would always come downstairs around half past seven to come and watch her favourite T.V programme and after it had finished she would go straight back upstairs. For Annika it was utmost imperative that every moment she lived her life corresponding with her age, her life had to revolve around doing something useful thus as she was 17 her sole time was dedicated wholly to doing her A levels. Everyday after school at approximately half five she would go straight upstairs to her bedroom after making her parents food and leaving it in the microwave, to do her school work. When she had cooked her parent's food and sniffed the luscious odour she would quote "smell of India". There was magic in Annika's hands because every time the Manda's had guests over they would compliment her authentic cooking saying how delicious it was. Her cousin once said "you're definitely going to make a perfect housewife one day" Annika would shy away from the comment and thought about the day she would leave from her house to live and rule her own life nurturing and understanding her own children, not a harshly as her father, and trusting her own parenting.

Tony walked into the lounge that evening, he gave a deplorable snarl at Sheena but she didn't even take any notice of him anymore. Both Sheena and Annika went into the kitchen to get out of the upcoming upheaval, they would smile and talk to each other happily like nothing had happened however, Annika horribly knew Tony was watching them both. It was like he had eyes at the back of his head.

Chapter 9

Rita started to become unnoticed nowadays she always kept to herself but she had to maintain the traditional wife belief where she couldn't hesitate to serving her husband, such as preparing his evening tea, ironing his clothes, all the normal menial tasks that were innate once you married if you were Indian. Even though Rita was living a nightmare for the past 30 years of her marriage, she still loved Tony, but sometimes she regretted the day she married him. This was because at times Annika would interrupt Rita when she was talking to God about her life and what the years ahead held for her, she prayed for a happy and peaceful family and then she would begin to cry, but it was difficult for Annika or the others to give her that support she needed.

Behind Closed Doors

Annika would sympathise with her mum and provided all the care and support she could but even at times Rita treated Annika in a harsh manner, for example if Annika didn't hear what her mum had told her to do, Rita and Tony in return would mutter "don't know where her mind has gone nowadays, it's like Sheena is corrupting her and she is just tagging along with her, she'll be just like, her imitation." This made Annika really upset and guilty but her way of thinking was that they said these things so that she was pre aware before taking the step of having a boyfriend, despite the fact that it became a constant network of comments everyday. In conclusion the question was whether Annika was affected by this because there was no sense of resentment towards her parents. As usual Annika questioned herself to God, this time it was "why can't I speak to my own sister? I'm not going to go against her for what she did."

It was becoming a repeated method of asking questions to her God whilst she worshipped since these were inseparable moments. In continuation, she doubtfully said "Tony still meets his own sister who is an evil witch; she caused intricately much sorrow in this family especially to my mum." Furthermore she persisted to say "So why can't you get rid of her? But dad just goes and meets her after work without telling us when he knows full well how much uproar she caused in our family."

It is known in Asian cultures that your father's sister had to be the one who caused too much trouble in your family.

She thought back to year 2000 when Aunt Paula who was Tony's sister induced horrific pain and devastation in Annika's family. Aunt Paula was six foot tall, and her skin was dark, you could tell by her appearance that she had the devil's cold blue blood, pumping through her veins; moreover she was being excessively nice to Tony's children whom knew of her spiteful and cunning tricks. She tried to sway them to believe that their mum was manipulative. In year 2000 one evening at their house Aunt Paula had claimed that Rita had stirred up lies to Aunt Paula's older brother's wife. This was no where near the truth, it was evil Paula who was bang out of order because she planned the rumours and falsely accused Rita. Rita's children were more than sure that their mother wouldn't even dare cause such uproar, which would be shore to agitate her husband in an inhumane manner.

Chapter 10

Annika stopped immediately because it was getting late bearing in mind it was time for Annika to cook her granddad's evening meal just as she did everyday, since she learnt and was taught how to cook. She thought that Sheena was downstairs why couldn't she make it for a change, looking at her religious shrine at the same time. Once she had cooked her Granddad's meal she felt really tired so she decided to have an early night because she had school the next morning and her usual time to go to sleep would be around eleven o'clock in the night.

The alarm started to bleep at seven o' clock the next morning, Annika woke in an instance like it was a scene in a horror movie because usually in horror movies when the villain dies you would think he/she is dead but after a few moments they awake instantly and when the camera remains stationery on their faces, unpredictably their eyes open widely. Adi used to make fun of Annika because in the past every morning when her alarm went off she would wake up immediately like a robot. Once Adi played a trick on her it was on a weekend and Annika set her alarm for 10 o'clock, Adi stupidly woke Annika up purposely saying "you're late for school it's 9 o'clock" Annika woke up without knowing and started to get ready for school, a few moments later she realised that she was taken for a fool.

From this, you could adopt that Annika was very vigilant and organised, for this reason her punctuality and attendance at school was frequently 100%, yet she was still naïve and vulnerable enough, to sometimes slip, and let the people closest to her, take advantage of her. Apparently so, as Annika hypothesised those who start early in using their positive beliefs and morals in their own life taking into account how it affects their surroundings, this person then gives themselves the opportunity to strive for success or that fortune would be pre placed upon them. Annika could be contemplated into this assumption as she was the one who suggested this. With this thought, so often crossing her mind, it was hard not to see, why she wouldn't carry on, and take everyday in her stride. With such a positive outlook on life, yet such a different reality, Annika continued to have faith, with a possibility, that these so called luxuries, would fall upon her.

Life revolving around Annika was somewhat special, every step she would take was like a new snap shot added to her album. When she left for school every morning she would leave the house at about 8am then she would meet her best mate whose name was Rebecca. They would both walk to the bus stop and wait around 10 minutes for the bus to arrive. Rebecca was a lovely looking girl, she had a blend of brown and black hair which suited her very much and she also had an understanding and sincere character. They had both known each other for over 12 years. Because they lived closely to each other, at times after school in their back yards they would shout out each others names knowing they got home safely.

When Annika and Rebecca got to school each morning they would usually reach school about half past eight in the morning, this was good timing because registration didn't start until quarter to nine. After registration lessons would start at until quarter to nine, because they were in sixth form they only attended their lessons when they were due. Annika was in her first year of doing her AS Levels therefore each AS level accounted for five hours of lesson time each week. Annika studied three AS levels hence she only came to school for 15 hours per week and the rest of her 10 hours were for private study. The reason why Annika opted to do three AS levels was because she had decided to do work experience at the time, however after Sheena's incident Tony told her to quit her work experience, as a result she had Wednesday's free to do any extra study needed. The sacrifice she had to take was unfortunate for Annika, as this work experience would have given her the skills and abilities she needed to do finance in the future. Sadly Tony didn't understand her commitments and only saw the short term benefits not Annika's long term prospects. To look on the bright side she gained at least one months experience which was worthwhile but not the expected duration, this also kept her from regretting what she felt was her fault. When she was doing her experience she fitted well in the work place, all the colleagues were over 21 at least and she was the youngest one in the department, everyone was well-mannered and pleasant towards her. On the other hand Annika was the shy girl who wasn't as outspoken about her sociable life, even though she wasn't knowledgeable in that subject area, so whenever she did speak it was always regarding the work. Once she had left, her explanation was that she had education and family commitments.

Nevertheless, Annika used her free Wednesdays as private study, and perhaps this was the difference between a minority of her friends, as many of them didn't use private study usefully, but she thought they would do well so they didn't need the extra time they had. At school her closest friends were Rebecca, Katrina, Monica, Kim, Heena and Vicky the list just went on, however all of them were very intelligent. Annika was the oldest out of her friends so they all respected and listened to her, she wasn't a girl who you could argue with or create any enemies with this was because she had such a forgiving and naive personality which made you remorseful if you ever did have an argument. A classic example was when Annika accidentally stepped on her friends toe, her name was Katrina. Annika had told Katrina to step back on her foot because she was very superstitious that if she didn't she would get bad luck. In Asian cultures this was seen as an ancestral ethos.

"Stepping on your foot is like stepping on God's foot" Katrina in return said Annika was absolutely astounded

"Katrina, why do you respect me so much?" Annika commented back

"Because you have a one in a million personality and that you are the most kindest and sensible girl I have ever met, you do everything conscientiously, sometimes I wish I was like you but that can never happen this is why I respect you." Annika hugged Katrina and said

"I still want you to step on my foot; otherwise I'll get the bad luck, would you want that?" Katrina then gently stepped back on Annika's foot. It was almost like Katrina had an exaggerated perspective of Annika, if you came to think about it. Do people really portray others in such a kind and decent opinion? Or was it a way of gaining self respect, in Annika's case Katrina really meant it. Yet this was what made Annika self determined and unique to others but as a whole in her own life. As long as Annika was self assured and content she didn't really need other people's opinions to live her life against as it was you as an individual who was going to make your life valuable. This didn't mean she didn't cherish her friend's views, it was acceptable to think what you felt as everyone had the chance to free speech. All she ever wished for was her parents to see her in an honest and polite behaviour just like her friends.

Chapter 11

The day at school for Annika passed on by as normal, it was the end of the day and Annika and Rebecca were walking home from the bus stop. When Annika came home from school she always had a terrible feeling before she got home, it was more like a fear of not wanting to go home and that she currently started to feel like she wanted to stay at school longer, which was many teenagers nightmare but for Annika it was a place where she felt protected and away from home. Whilst on there way home Annika watched two children and their parent's come out of a metallic blue car, when she watched them it reminded her of such a perfect and happy family and there was no sign of trouble within their family, she didn't hope that there would be to the family she watched, it was just a thought that crossed her mind, wishing that her family was happy as theirs. Sadly when she thought of her family in such a content manner it would be destroyed by something frightening.

"Annika" Rebecca said and started to nudge on Annika's shoulders

"What were you thinking of?"

"Oh nothing I was just looking at how nice that blue car was" Annika replied doubtfully. Rebecca walked on straight towards her house and said bye to Annika, she then waved back at her. When Annika got to her house and entered her key to open the house door she thought right back to the day in year 2000 when Aunt Paula caused so much conflict and Annika was helpless to put things right. In her case she could do nothing as she was only a young girl, what difference did it make when a child puts their opinion across in the Manda family or even in Indian families?

Perhaps in life people didn't consider that sometimes the younger generation actually were correct in telling the older generation that they were in the wrong and it was the younger generation who corrected them whenever it was needed to be done. In addition this was what Annika wanted to do in her family, to tell Tony how wrong he was when he remarked unjustified comments at either her or Sheena.

She ran straight upstairs to her bedroom when she opened the front door. On her comfy bed Annika sat there thinking of the haunting day in her house in the year 2000. This day caused a huge amount of devastation and slander that was appointed upon Rita and Tony cursing all kinds of expletives towards Rita. Aunt Paula was the one to blame for the upheaval, she was the one who manipulated and indoctrinated Tony with complete lies about Rita. Annika sat in her room on her comfy bed, she lay down and closed her eyes thinking about Aunt Paula, what such an evil cow she was, how did humans become so cruel? And why did they cause dilemmas in other families?

"I want a divorce, my solicitor has the papers ready, matter of fact I'll ring him now to get them prepared" Tony shouted at Rita.

He went to grab the phone and started to dial up his solicitor's number, as he did this Annika followed him and tried stopping him, but he fumed at her with so much disgust that she backed away. You could tell he didn't even ring him; it was a false phone call because he only pressed a few buttons and he only said on the phone "get the papers ready" and put the phone down. What solicitor would recognise Tony's voice quickly unless the solicitor was expecting it? It was done so quickly that not even when Tony dialled the number it would have connected in such a fast pace. All because of petty Paula, for some reason she was jealous of Rita, somehow she wanted Tony to get rid of her. But Rita was like a titan, she had all the strength to overthrow the likes of Aunt Paula and stopped her marriage from falling apart she had done it for the past 30 years and nothing prevented her from doing it again.

Tony and Rita's marriage had experienced a lot of arguments and clashes, the foundation that their marriage was built on 30 years ago didn't even shake. Even though the above surface fell to pieces due to the arguments, still the foundation didn't collapse. This was because it consisted of love, commitment and shackles it was these three components that kept their marriage in a strong bond no matter of all the thorns it may have suffered from, it didn't allow for their marriage to be affected. This was Annika's perception of her parent's marriage but most importantly one day when she marries it will be a foundation that she will have to build.

Annika didn't realise she was lying on her bed for an hour now, after thinking about the unforgettable incident four years ago, she decided since Sheena revealed her relationship with Ashley there will be no more arguments. This time she meant it, it was the only way her family would be blissful again. Yet, she knew behind close doors there was a story to tell for every family in the world, there was no such thing as a perfect family, no matter how hard you tried to keep up to idyllic norms.

Chapter 12

On the same day, Aunt Paula had invited Tony's family for dinner. Annika was 100% sure that she was going to stay at home and so was Rita.

"Why should we go to that conniving snakes house, she's a bloody phoney, she's using you and you are blinded by her sisterly love. Well, Tony none of our children will be going with you. You can't trust what she might do, don't forget about what she did four years ago to our family!" Rita exclaimed. Tony was shocked to hear what Rita had said; he sat down completely speechless this was because it was the truth.

"It's great when the truth is bitter, now look at you, reduced to sit lower otherwise you would mouth at me and the kids, this time I'm not letting that cunning cow take you and my family for a ride." Rita continued to say, she then walked straight out of the room and slammed the door behind her causing a minute shake in the house. Annika was amazed by the fact that Rita had finally spoke back to Tony, otherwise she would sit quietly like a puppy and not say a word.

"Go on mum, you did a great job, I'm glad you showed him your strength and shut his gob before giving the third degree about Aunt Paula" Annika said after following Rita into the lounge.

"I hope so, this time we are not letting Paula win, and she bloody gets what she wants by manipulating your father, then she just uses him and leaves him behind when it comes to family occasions. Sometimes I wish God punished her somehow. She is a growing thorn in this family and the only way to obliterate her is the truth about what she really is like inside to Tony." Rita was full of zeal and eagerness to do something about Aunt Paula but it wasn't good for Rita to think in such a vengeance manner as it ruined her kindness within.

That same night Tony still went to Aunt Paula's house, he needed to learn how to say no and not fear his own flesh and blood. To the outside world Tony put on a superficial front but behind close doors, he was a stubborn and terrified man who couldn't face the music of his own side of the family consisting of malevolent people. On the other hand, because Tony went alone to Aunt Paula's the rest of the family had no idea what they would say behind their backs.

Tony was too submissive and listened frequently to his sister without even disputing her opinion. Again Annika thought that a lot of things happened behind close doors. On many occasions whenever Tony visited Aunt Paula's house, afterwards when he came home he acted like a completely changed man but it wasn't good, normally he would start to argue with Rita shouting all kinds of odds at Rita and how she was a burden to his side of the family the day he got married to her. Thus, Annika knew whenever he came back from Aunt Paula's house he would be intoxicated with alcohol and definitely start a rift with Rita whom was never in the wrong. Following that night Tony got home just before one o'clock in the morning acting tipsy which was expected, he was dropped off by one of Aunt Paula's son. When he came into the house it was completely pitch black because everyone had gone to sleep, Annika was awake in her bed and she listened to her dad come up the stairs making growling noises and talking to himself. As he went straight into his bedroom Rita was fast asleep, he switched the light on causing Rita to twitch by the glow of light in the room, she noticed Tony was here but she ignored him and went back to sleep. Tony pushed Rita and pulled her blanket, Rita spoke tiredly "what are you doing can't you see I am asleep just because you can't see others peaceful you stop me from having my sleep". From that point on Tony begun to yell in hostility, he just kept repeating the same old stuff from the past and making himself come down to tears. Rita sat in her bed listening to Tony's lecture; he continued to replicate the same words against Rita because he had no reason to make a new argument. What he believed involved Rita's barbaric behaviour.

The next morning, Tony had gone off to work as usual leaving his lunch behind. Rita was shattered after last night's performance therefore she rang in sick at work.

"Mum, that's good you didn't go into work because you need all the rest you can get. Dad is so blind to see what he is doing to you. Sometimes I think Aunt Paula has done something to dad, he is brainwashed by there opinions about us, which makes him go against us every time he goes to see her…… Anyways I'll see you later mum I'm off to school now, make sure you stay in bed and take some medication if you have to." Annika said to her mum. "Okay sweetie, bye." Rita replied watching her daughter leave the room.

At school Annika studied her A levels. She did three A levels that involved subjects related to business studies and psychology. In Indian cultures it was a typical stereotype for a plethora of Asians to take an A level relating to business studies. Hence, Annika enjoyed her subjects very much; she didn't really have a favourite subject this was because she concentrated in doing well in all her areas of study. However, she hoped to further

her future career into psychology or maybe accounting. Tony always wanted Annika to do accounting when she grew older, therefore Annika maintained her father's wish and also identified her other area of interest which was psychology. In this case she didn't fail to sustain Tony's aspiration as she knew Tony was her father, after all he wanted the best for her. Annika only ever did for others, but she kept forgetting to achieve her own ambitions, at the age of 17 she had the mind and attitude of a very responsible adult, carrying everyone else's weight on her shoulders.

Chapter 13

The month of December was coming to an end, more like a disastrous December this was because to end it the Manda family had to face the Christmas and the New Year season. In Annika's case she was really happy to have Christmas and the New Year come around so quickly because she felt it was this time of the year that will bring her family together to start a fresh. However, everyone in the family were all in a sorrowing mood after Sheena's great big secret was revealed and Tony still being best chums with his sister. Nobody this time round decided to put up the Christmas tree and decorations, but it was Annika who was up for a great Christmas because no one else was in the mood of a Christmas spirit. Annika gathered herself to bring down the Christmas tree and beautify it with all her favourite white tinsel and baubles, the tree was at least six foot in height. She felt this was the only way to keep her family happy and be united before the New Year. To add enhancement to the tree she added multicoloured fairy lights which lit up the whole of the lounge to give it that extra touch. It took her about 2 hours to complete the tree and the end result was definitely worth it, the tree looked absolutely amazing, nobody could top Annika's style of dressing a Christmas tree; to put the icing on the cake she added a glittering white star.

When it came to Christmas Eve which landed on a Saturday Annika had to go to work. The restaurant was crowded with herds of people especially at lunch time; everyone came for the special Christmas lunch which was two slices of juicy turkey, golden roast potatoes, spicy stuffing, mixed vegetables with luscious gravy and cranberry sauce, the sauce was optional though, the additional dessert was Christmas pudding and it came to a affordable price, this was why there were so many people queuing for the Christmas lunch. Annika thought to herself why people would spend so much money just to have the Christmas lunch; thinks exactly like a traditional Indian, couldn't they make it at home. But then she thought she gets paid for doing her job, if nobody came to the restaurant where would the money come from.

At work Annika was close friends with Holly, they both got on really well and they both did their jobs correctly and responsibly. Annika and Holly would make foolish comments about the other girls who worked with them this was because they didn't do much work. Frequently they stood around chatting about what they did during the week and when they were going to meet up next. Usually they would expect Annika and Holly to do the work whilst they stood around talking, which was really uptight of them to do. Nonetheless Annika never bothered with them, as she remained the certainty it was her part-time job where she would make the money and then move on when she needed to. After, she would never see those girls again. Due to the Christmas period it meant that Annika had to finish work later than usual, it was only by an extra hour late in which she got paid for. As it was a Saturday, the dishes were double than normal and it was this part of the job that was the most time consuming because first you had to put them in the dishwasher, after four minutes you would have to dry and stack them and once this was done the dishes had to be put back to their regular positions. As you expected, it was Annika and Holly who did the stacking and washing of the dishes, this was beneficial to the restaurant as they worked efficiently in a team to get the job done properly and quickly as an opposed to the others who would have done it much more slowly.

It was around half six when Annika got home from work the evening had come to an end, without Annika even noticing since she was at work and, being the winter season therefore it was much darker outside when it struck six o'clock. Every time Annika got home from work especially on a Saturday her feet would ache in so much pain particularly from the toes and the back of her foot. Her job involved her to stand up all day and walk back and forth, but her favourite part was remaining on the till because it not only added to her numerical skills it also meant she stood in one position rather than moving from one place to the next. Annika preserved the morale within herself including her philosophy which went something like this starting your first job young which was at the age of 16 was your first step to success and maturity for the future. Therefore, commencing your job at 16 provided you with the ability to increase your skills in self determination and thinking industrious will give you a head start facing the reality of work life and what it will be like for your ideal career. Moreover, you will have a healthy bank balance when you turn 21. Hence, providing such a valuable incentive for 16 year olds to start their first job at 16, taking into account the current economics with inflation rising and house prices booming all the finance they build young will be useful for future responsibilities.

It was Christmas eve Tony and Rita had gone out for the evening, at home was Adi, Annika, Sheena, Kareena and their granddad whom remained in his bedroom majority of the day asleep. It was around half past seven and there was a knock at the door. Annika went to look who it was and she noticed it was Ashley. However, Adi went to open the door and Annika was about to stop him but he opened the door before she could get to him. Adi looked at the tall and pleasant looking guy standing in front of him Adi didn't seem to recognise him, Annika watched from behind and Kareena came running to see who was at the door when Kareena saw the young guy she knew it was Ashley straight away.

"Let me handle this Adi" Kareena said from behind.

"Why, who is it?" Adi replied

"Don't worry who it is, I'll sort everything, you just go inside"

"No, I want to know who it is, just tell me will you!" Adi became very curious and asked Annika if she knew who the guy was. She looked directly at him and said it was Ashley. Adi's face shone with shock, he went up to the front door and demanded him to go away or things would turn out to be nasty. Kareena stepped in and said to Adi

"will you stop being an idiot for once. I'll sort everything out in a civil manner you are just going to make things worse"

"Whatever, you'll just agree to what he will say; I'm the man of the family when dad's not here so budge over to the side"

"Adi, stop being ridiculous you know Kareena is the oldest; she'll talk to him respectively all you will do is make a big scene" Annika spoke. Ashley watched stunningly at Adi and Kareena arguing, without them noticing he walked away and drove off in his car, both Adi and Kareena only became aware of this when they heard his car start and drive off. Annika was glad that he had gone otherwise God knows what would have happened between Adi and Ashley.

Kareena shut the door and went directly into the lounge, Adi followed in by and so did Annika. Adi kept arguing with Kareena

"it's your entire fault he's gone; otherwise I would have stopped him from coming here ever again. How dare he even step a foot outside our house, who does he think he is? And you wanted to speak to him about Sheena's marriage have you gone mad? You know they can't get married so why were you even trying to be nice?"

"No I wasn't, why don't you shut your mouth, all I was going to do was tell him that dad will never agree because it would be breaking our traditions and then persuade him to get over Sheena" Kareena spoke back in great resentment.

"You are only saying that now because he has gone, I no your type sister supporting the other sister, including you as well Annika" Kareena became very angry that she picked up the empty glass next to her and chucked it at Adi, but she had missed her aim. The glass dropped into pieces causing an ear aching sound. After a few moments Sheena came running down the stairs from her room into the lounge.

Chapter 14

Sheena looked around the lounge in bewilderment.

"What happened here?" she said

"Don't act like you don't know, you know damn well what has happened matter of fact you are probably the one who planned this." Adi replied

"What are you talking about? I don't understand you"

"Stop acting all innocent, you told Ashley to come to our house and talk to mum and dad about your marriage with him, aren't you grateful that dad wasn't here? Otherwise you would have caused a feud"

"What you mean Ashley really came here? Oh my god I can't believe that he never comes here without my permission, I must contact him." Sheena stood in shock to hear Ashley had come to her house, she then ran upstairs to ring him off the house phone but it went straight to his voicemail. Meanwhile, Adi, Kareena and Annika were deciding whether Rita and Tony should come to know of this. Adi was very obdurate he was desperate to tell Tony about Ashley's unexpected appearance. However Annika and Kareena wanted it to be an incident that never happened so that it would pass. Kareena knew Adi would open his big mouth just to get Sheena in trouble again, so she was stuck in the middle as it was very difficult to control someone like Adi. Annika tried her best to stop Adi from telling Tony and Rita about the incident, but for Adi he saw this as advantage to sway Tony onto his side so that in return Tony would see a new side to Adi, a much more matured and moralistic boy.

Annika and Kareena knew nothing was going to stop Adi, but in some situations Adi only ever mocked around for a short period of time so that Annika and Kareena could start to get angrier. Sheena became more worried about Ashley because his phone was switched off, she thought that Adi might have threatened him or that he might end up doing something stupid because he really cared for her and not only he hadn't seen her for days now.

The clock ticked on by, it struck half nine in the evening Annika had cleaned the broken glass so that Tony and Rita didn't notice, Kareena was on the computer checking her emails, Sheena was upstairs lying on her bed and Adi was in his room. This was definitely a Christmas Eve to remember Annika thought sitting in the lounge. Rita and Tony had strolled in and Annika kept thinking what will happen next, therefore she ran upstairs to her room so that she didn't need to face any questions off Tony if he noticed something suspicious. Soon as they walked in Adi came running down from his room fired up, you could tell he had knocked back some of Tony's whiskey before he faced Tony and Rita.

In Adi's books he told everyone that he didn't drink alcohol but this was the biggest white lie he ever told. Surely a couple more lies were attached along his string. The reason he told everyone that he didn't drink was because Rita had built so much trust within him that he swore on Rita's life that he will never touch alcohol. But he has broken his mum's trust who will never forgive him if she ever came to know.

Annika rushed to open her door to stop Adi but once again he was too fast for her. She stood by the banister and listened to what Adi had to say. She was a very vigilant girl who listened and picked up every word Adi had spoken. As you could imagine he was bound to portray himself as the innocent and right one and denigrate Kareena. The picture was crystal clear he had indoctrinated Tony and Rita, and he scorned Kareena out of the picture. Annika knew something had to be done otherwise Rita and Tony only heard half the story not even that. Whilst Kareena was checking her emails without anticipation Tony blasted out her name

"KAREENA, come here now!" you could hear the coarse tone in his voice.

Kareena shut down the computer and walked to the lounge, Annika came running down nodding her head at Kareena, giving the impression to Kareena that Adi had told Rita and Tony about Ashley. Kareena entered the lounge with Annika behind her and Tony was standing in front like a brick wall.

"Kareena you are the oldest right? So why don't you act like one even Adi has more sense than you"

"well, let me guess Adi has drilled into your minds totally different stories to the truth, how can you lot be so vulnerable to Adi's lies? I am not going to waste my energy and time on a little twat like him and I'll tell you straight dad what I did was right, I tried explaining to Ashley that Sheena couldn't marry him because it was against our tradition and religion."

If you are confused, here is an example, in the Christian religion there are many castes for instance Catholics. This applies to all the other religions where a caste system is constructed from many years ago. Therefore in the Manda family because they were Indians the same rules applied to them, they weren't meant to marry out of caste in which Ashley was.

Fortunately this was an ancestral belief however, Tony lived with this custom and he was assured that he would pass this on to the next generation in his family.

In turn Kareena said to Adi "you are such an idiot, why can't you explain the truth rather than making yourself look good in front of mum and dad"

"is this true Adi are you telling lies about your sister?" Tony interrupted Kareena

"no I am not, was I wrong in trying to stop Kareena from talking to Ashley so that she could agree to him?

"how many times I wasn't agreeing to him, I was going to tell him the truth, but your big headed behaviour caused him to go away. Dad, can't you see he is blinding you with lies, he is trying to act blameless so that you could start to believe he has become sensible and more responsible"

"I don't care what the truth is; you shouldn't have opened the door in the first place. Now Adi I know your type and I know you fully well. You could never act responsible with the attitude you have so don't try acting smart with me. Now both of you get upstairs and let's forget this happened its Christmas Eve remember." Tony said with a sense of content.

They all headed upstairs besides Annika. She sat in the lounge thinking how much of a hypocrite Adi was because he had a list of girlfriends who were not the same religion but it was okay for him to criticise Sheena.

Chapter 15

In Indian cultures the ancient belief was boys were seen as princes and girls were seen as burdens. This was why Adi wasn't taunted for his faults. Daughters in Indian families knew it was almost inevitable that one day they will marry and go to their husband's house. Regrettably, this was why girls were treated very restrictively as their in-laws didn't want disobedient daughter in-laws. On the contrary this had vanished many years ago but in Tony's case this ethos still lived. Tony always indoctrinated his daughters that they could never have a boyfriend and marry someone of their own choice. Adi was brought up with the same belief however, Tony didn't worry as much for him as others saw girls going astray humiliating for the family they came from. Further it would become a hot topic to discuss in Asian families if Indian girls walked around in public with their boyfriends displaying their affection. Contemporarily this norm was diminishing because parents knew times had changed that even Indian girls were pregnant under age. Hence it was similar to the idea that if a girl walked around town with a child someone would suspect it was theirs without even knowing if it was really theirs or whether they were just looking after the child.

It was horrible to have such an bounded life, this was the way Kareena, Sheena, Annika, Adi and even Rita felt, it was like they were living in prison, they could have no sense of freedom. The Manda family were such a perfect family from the outside but behind close doors it was a different story altogether. It was mainly Tony's fault for making his family to be perceived as immaculate. He wanted to keep up to expectations so that no one could criticise him and his family. This was why he was very fearful that his children would step out of line. Tony didn't realise that keeping them strained made them more likely to cross his limits.

Chapter 16

Christmas Eve had ended abruptly and with the surprising turn up of Ashley. The next day was a bright and cheery morning, just right for a Sunday Christmas morning. But in the Manda's house it was the complete opposite, no one got up from bed until 12 noon. Annika was happy as a hyena because it was her first Sunday off from work, so she could get a proper lie in. Every night Annika would sleep with her curtains half open, so when she woke up for the next morning a strip of bright sunshine glistened on her face to wake her up. She had her own bedroom with her own double bed so that when she did wake up she woke up with great ease looking directly through the window to the beautiful outside world. When she woke up she saw the trees swaying side by side against the forceful wind and white snowflakes moving directly to the right, she rushed out of bed and opened her curtains to see the shimmering snow.

It was snowing on Christmas day Annika couldn't believe her eyes; this was because it hardly ever snowed on Christmas day. She then decided to go back into bed for another half an hour the snow made her think of all the comforts in life and she only imagined her life to be as comforting as she thought but the havoc from last night destroyed this consideration. It was almost inevitable that today would be disastrous just like the other Christmases, full of boredom and watching the movies that came on the television to make the day pass. Annika still felt a bit tired and all she wanted to do was spend Christmas tucked up in her comfy bed, without realisation she fell asleep. It wasn't until half an hour; Rita came into Annika's room and told her to wake up.

"Have you seen the snow out there it is at least 12 inches deep" Rita exclaimed. Annika moaned a little and tiredly said "let me have some more sleep, I'll get up in the bit"

"Now, now it's Christmas day and you don't want to spend it in bed, we have to get the Christmas lunch ready, it's just after 1 o' clock so pop your clothes on so that we can get the dinner started"

"Okay I'll be down in 10" she replied under her blanket.

After a few moments Annika got out of bed and went straight to the bathroom, she splashed her face with lukewarm water pouring out of the tap and looked directly into the mirror.

"What an ugly face" she said and gave a little chuckle. Annika was never confident about her appearance; she wore glasses and always tied her hair back mainly to comply with her fathers will

At school because of her appearance and unforgettable personality people assumed her to be very clever and a good girl. Annika definitely was clever but she told herself that she wasn't too intelligent or too dumb she was just average for her intelligence level. Nonetheless, there was something always unknown that made her different from other girls and this was her morals. One of them was that you didn't need beauty to be successful in life, but sometimes in some situations it might be essential.

For instance, Annika went for a job interview for an established fashion company about a month ago, when she attended the interview she was up against 6 other rivals who wanted the same position and the company was only offering two places. Before she went to the interview she did her research on the company, it was summarised to be a sensational and glamorous fashion icon, despite this she still went for the job. For Annika it wasn't fitting into the sexy cliché world of the company it was for a vacancy as a retail advisor and gaining experience. The interview consisted of many role plays with the others and an individual interview with the interviewer. However, one imminent detail Annika noticed was that the interviewer focussed mainly on the very pretty girls. In the end she didn't get the job, just to assure oneself, she went to the fashion department for the position she applied for and surprisingly the two girls who the interviewer focused on got the job. Thus, it justifies her belief, yet it's not the case for all circumstances, this is why you shouldn't '*judge a book by its cover*' as it is said.

Downstairs in the kitchen Rita was getting the food ready, Annika came down to help her mother, she noticed the luscious turkey and the seasonal vegetables which were fresh as the bright morning. Rita began to carve the turkey into thin slices and Annika added the complementary food items on the patterned plates. Whilst they were busy in the kitchen everyone came down stairs and sat by the dining table as they knew lunch was ready from the dreamy smell. Annika got the entire cutlery ready and placed them on the table in a formal format. Soon after, everyone was tucking into their Christmas dinner without a single word said. Once everyone had eaten, Annika hoped for the rest of the day to end peacefully. Tony was upstairs in the bathroom however he came rushing down after a couple of minutes, he came into the lounge and mouthed off about pieces of hair been cut and left around the basin. In the family it was always Adi who cut his hair and left his cut hair in the bathroom basin. It was like Tony had an obsessive compulsive disorder to keep everything clean because of this he started to give the third degree at Adi for his manner less doings.

"Flipping heck, I'm your only bloody son and you are always trying to find faults in me. This is why you can't get us to love you and appreciate you as our father. You always keep us like we are your prisoners and that you have complete control over us"

"don't start your only son business; the girls have equal importance as well as you." Unexpectedly Rita breaks the argument

"Can't you lot just keep quiet, it's Christmas day for God's sake" she says. Ignoring Rita both of them kept on arguing for another hour or so by the time Christmas day was coming to an end. Unsurprisingly, it was another Christmas from hell for the Manda family.

Chapter 17

The New Year was just around the corner, Annika was hoping that it would be a good one this time round, but with obvious reasons it probably would be a chaotic one. Therefore, you couldn't blame the way Annika thought it was more or less unavoidable to think in this way. You might have gathered that everything is falling apart for the Manda family, not just the family but their home and image as well. Tony begun to think that his once perfect family was now crumbling to pieces. All the secrets begun to unravel in front of him in which he didn't have control to stop them from happening. He is beginning to judge the way he nurtured his children and whether his upbringing lacked something that has caused him to see these days. Because of Tony's controlling method when his children were small he didn't allow them to mix with their first cousins whom were his nieces and nephews. Sheena would blame this on Tony because now his children were very much distant from them considering they only lived about 15 minutes away in car.

It was Boxing Day and Annika had to work bearing in mind she did get paid time and a half, so it was beneficial for her. As usual the day was busy at the restaurant so time flew before you knew it. When Annika was at work she would look at her watch and think this is going to be a very long and tiring day. However, her solution to time passing on by much quicker was by not looking at her watch until she estimated 2 hours had gone by, and then when she looked at her watch it was nearer to the end of the day. Working at the restaurant wasn't Annika's ideal job, but a job was a job so no matter if you she didn't enjoy it she still was getting paid. Annika was now 18 years old therefore she had been working in the restaurant for nearly 2 years now.

The next day, Rita had gone up town to purchase snacks and other essentials for the New Year, it wasn't anything special, just some odd things that were needed to celebrate the New Year at the Manda's. The days hurried on by towards the New Year Annika sat in her bedroom on the floor speaking to her God "it was for the best life was going fast, not only because I can't wait to grow older but also it meant that Sheena's situation will be swept away and forgotten about." It made her introspect about what would happen next year about Sheena. This was because even though Sheena wanted to leave the house and Tony shouted at her to leave he still would stop her from leaving. It seemed Tony was in denial and the reason he stopped Sheena from leaving, despite him saying to her to leave he didn't want people from outside humiliate him and his family as he had built a recognisable status for himself for having a pleasant family.

Whilst Annika was sitting on her bedroom floor she felt the bubbles in her carpet, her carpet was a bright blue colour which was only just recently replaced from her old carpet which was a mouldy green colour. The mouldy green carpet flooded a lot of memories back to Annika this is because her bedroom experienced the most arguments Tony and Rita ever had. Since Adi and Annika were in elementary school and Kareena and Sheena were in high school Tony used to constantly argue with Rita, it was absolutely terrifying for Adi and especially for Annika because they were only about 5 or 6 years of age when they had to hear Tony's vilification of Rita.

When you are young your parents are the most important people in your life, however this could have been the reason why the Manda children drifted away from Tony and were much more fearful of him. For Rita having a divorce from Tony was very difficult. In Asian cultures if your marriage was in jeopardy a divorce would be the last resort, no matter how many times you tried to make your marriage work. Likewise your reputation would be stained forever, because in the future if you decided to marry again, the person who you will marry will think twice to why you ended up getting divorced in the first place.

Despite what Rita has been through for the past years, she still loves Tony and if she did leave him, all that would be at the back of her mind is what will happen to Tony if he was left alone? This is because he was really dependant on his family. Annika also knew that if Rita left Tony, he would become very isolated and depressed and that the rest of his life would be lived catastrophically predominated by his side of the family. Who would continue to indoctrinate him especially Aunt Paula who despised Rita.

Chapter 18

"5….4….3…..2…..1 Happy New Year" everyone in the Manda family shouted when the Big Ben struck 12 o'clock midnight on the television. Every year round on T.V the media would broadcast the vibrant and colourful fireworks display in London so that the whole of Britain was entertained for at least ten minutes. This made Annika look forward to tomorrow, a new fresh start to another year. Annika was continuously messaging on her phone but she couldn't even send any messages because of all the networks being down. This was due to the networks being relentlessly jammed with so many people text messaging. It was a good idea to text early because this was a common occurrence every year for the mobile networks to get jammed.

At the Manda's the New Year was celebrated in a mundane manner, only ever a few words were exchanged despairingly. When Adi said Happy New Year to Tony he said it disappointingly however when he said it to Rita, it was said in a much happier and enthusiastic tone. Nevertheless Annika didn't express this divide between her parents, when she did say Happy New Year to Tony she said it excitingly and in the same way to Rita. Just as you thought not another argument, actually there wasn't one, so it was great for Annika to experience a day peacefully, but it wasn't great fun when the clock did strike 12 o'clock either.

To end 2005 and to begin 2006, always remember that even though the sunset has gone down making you feel hopeless, never feel this way because after a sunset there is always a sunrise hence, new hope and another chance to start a fresh. Also consider this because it helps you take that step forward to your destination in life.

Chapter 19

2006, Annika thought to herself, she loved the fact that life was going fast and she couldn't wait to grow older and have her own independent life. That was what she wanted her independency, it was difficult as you could imagine for anybody living with a father like Tony to gain such autonomy. However, because Tony ruled an authoritarian parenting style upon his children this was passed onto his children to be self disciplined when they did have their own control. Fortunately for Annika 2006 was her final year for her A levels, so that when it did come to June she would be undertaking her final examinations. She hesitated at the thought of her final exams, yet with self confidence she knew she would do well because she had been revising and doing extra revision for her A levels. Her input into her education was immeasurable as a result her immense effort should pay off at the end of it.

It had been over a year now since Tony found out about Sheena's relationship with Ashley and things were going accordingly for the Manda's. Tony's perception of Sheena's situation was that she had forgotten about Ashley and moved on with her life. Most of all, Tony knew this time round he got himself lucky because he got away without getting humiliated. Sadly, he was wrong because Sheena was still meeting Ashley without him knowing. Sheena's attitude was very dire towards Tony; she still had not forgiven him since the day she told him about her relationship with Ashley. Her past meetings with Ashley conveyed her lack of fear from Tony and most of all her love for Ashley, she still maintained the hope they will be together forever and that she would never allow for her long relationship with him to go down the drain.

From the old myths it was known that in every family there was the quiet one and the wild one. Likewise for the Manda's it was Sheena who was the wild one of the family and surprisingly Kareena was the quiet one. You might have expected Annika to be the shy and the quiet one however, she was shy but this was only short-term. Annika could have been classified as the intelligent one. Ever since Sheena was in her teens she tended to be the very detached from the family and grew up in her own way of thinking. She inherited her temper from Tony and her talkative habit off Rita. Irrespective of Sheena's heavy attitude, for an Asian girl to be strong headed from young was beneficial for their self defence as the world was not a safe place anymore. In many occasions Sheena taught Annika how to be defensive for any fearing situation. She always told her to keep her key or a pen in her pocket for any unexpected occurrences in which she could immediately stab a potential criminal in the thigh. In addition Sheena taught her how to kick a guy down below if needs be.

It was very difficult to live a lie for Annika, this was because she knew that Sheena still wanted to be with Ashley for more reason this made it complex for Annika to face her father when knowing the truth. In a way Annika was stuck in the middle, she upheld the belief that Sheena was a grown woman therefore Tony didn't need to control her life and it was up to Sheena to choose her life partner.

As the days mounted towards the end of the month, Annika had experienced a huge pile of remarks from her parents. This was because Annika got on well with Sheena therefore Tony observed there relationship in which he felt it was wrong for Annika to mix with her own sister and that Annika should have got on with Kareena who was becoming invisible these days. Most of the days when Sheena came late from work Tony still doubted that she was up to no good however, he couldn't question without any assurance. One evening, Annika was sitting in the lounge with her parents, they heard the front door close after 6 o'clock in the evening, and Tony had mumbled a few words to Rita

"She's starting to come late from work, I hope she isn't meeting Ashley behind our backs" and when he said this comment he looked directly at Annika assuming she would know. For Annika it was largely hurtful for her parents to think in this way, because she didn't believe that Sheena was wrong and that falling in love with someone was the first step to finding your right life partner. Annika logically debated to oneself that if Tony still met with his sister whom was a conniving cow and horrible to Rita why was it inadequate for her to talk to her own sister.

Chapter 20

Annika was gradually counting the days towards her examinations excluding her weekends. She had been revising for months on end now so hopefully she would do exceptionally well. The next couple of months fast forwarded by because it was the same old routine to follow when it came to living under the roof of the Manda's house. Hence, as the days ended it came to Annika's final day at school before she headed off for study leave and she would have only came into school to undertake her examinations. Annika reminisced back to year 1999, when she started high school she could remember getting lost in such a huge school, all her nerves were building up because she was the new kid in school. But she didn't worry because Adi was in the same school so he would have supported her if there was any trouble; however Annika was always a good girl whom didn't get into any fights or arguments.

The one memory she will always cherish is her first crush, she was only 14 when she became affectionately attracted to a boy who was 2 years older than her. The first time she set eyes on him was at the end of school time. Rebecca had noticed this tall handsome and innocent looking guy, before Annika had noticed him, Rebecca told Annika that there is this guy who she definitely knew Annika would fall for. Rebecca told her to look on her far left hand side to where the boy was standing with a few of his friends and giggling away. She remembered the exact words Rebecca had said to her

"Are you dazzled by his fair yellow skin, his tall handsome height and his gorgeous smile?" Annika was completely mesmerised that everything around her was silent and she was living on *cloud 9*, after a few moments she came out of her illusion and commented back to Rebecca

"Oh my God, he is so good looking and no doubt he has a fabulous personality, just the perfect guy for me." For 2 years until she reached the end of 16 years old Annika admired this charming looking guy until she felt it was time to move on. Furthermore, after the two years she knew there was no point in fancying the guy she liked because she knew there was no destination to this phase. Annika kept kidding herself because she knew *absence made the heart grow fonder* so in Annika's situation it was the distance that kept her attraction attached to him.

Generally Annika was unfortunate when it came to admiring a boy but she didn't bother much in this topic because not only she knew she couldn't have a boyfriend as her father was strict also she wasn't confident within herself when appearance was standing in front of her.

"ANNIKA" someone shouted from behind, Annika turned around and noticed it was Serene.
"Can't believe it's our last day at school, it just feels like we started yesterday." Serene dubiously said.
"I know we have to move on one day, that's what life revolves around, moving forward we can't turn back the clock" she said looking at the bright sky "that's true but we all have to stay in touch especially you and Rebecca we all started high school together and now we have to commence a new journey from scratch", "you got it" Annika muttered and moved her head to the left at the same time "well let's not get sad, everyone's inside having their lunch together and making the most of their time together, come and join us" Serene laughed
"yeah I'll be there in the minute you go on by",
"are you sure you are okay?" "Yes I'm fine" she falsely said.

Annika glanced at the concrete floor surrounding her and watching the little kids play their games and having fun. Then she looked across to the skyscraper buildings remembering the times she used to have lessons in there. When she went back inside everyone was taking photos for memories, as she watched all her good memories came flushing back to her that made her want to cry but she disguised her feelings.

Chapter 21

When the day came to a close, everyone in Annika's year was saddened and Annika and most of her friends were in tears. It was such a heartbreaking moment but they all kept the faith that they will never lose contact with each other. After, everyone had said their goodbyes Annika, Rebecca and Serene walked up to their bus stop along with everyone else. The bus stop was approximately ten minutes away.

"Well guys this is the last day together" Serene sadly said

"Let's not get unhopeful, we must spend the last day at school cheerfully and remember we still have the prom to look forward to after the exams" Annika happily said and hugged Serene at the same time. Whilst they walked to the bus stop, Annika was two minded about leaving her high school. She felt happy on the one side but miserable on the other, she thought it was amazing that she could be feeling two emotions at the same time, which were the opposites. Once they got to the bus stop, she looked at all her friends and observed whether they would be feeling the same as her, however all of them articulated depressing expressions in which she was searching for happiness as well. Few moments later the bus arrived for Annika, Rebecca and Serene in which they caught to get home, the others waited for a different bus. As the bus came down the road everyone quickly hugged Annika, Serene and Rebecca before they got onto the bus. On the way home on the bus it was a moment that stunned Rebecca and Serene silently however, Annika was unresponsive. She then stated "come on guys I know it's sad a moment but look on the bright side least we will be saving money now from catching the bus to school." Annika tried her best to cheer the two up but it didn't work.

Annika was disheartened internally but she knew if she showed it, it would be difficult for her to face Serene and Rebecca and most importantly leave her high school.

Sometimes in life you have to let go of things so that you came move on in life but, for Annika, Rebecca and Serene it was too complex for them to do such a thing. Moreover, there are always benefits to this, whereas some people don't get the chance to move forward in life.

"Think about all those opportunities crying out to us, we might be blind to them now but we know they will always be there for us so we can take the step further and pursue our aspirations." Annika expressed in content.

"I suppose you are right" Serene replied back. Their journey on the bus was almost silent until Annika interrupted so she knew Rebecca and Serene were literally unhurt. When they got off the bus Annika told Serene to miss call her when she got home, to keep her mind at ease that she had got home safely. Annika and Rebecca walked home unspoken; when Rebecca came near to her house she embraced Annika upsettingly and said her goodbye. Annika was speechless but comforted Rebecca before she got home and she was content when Serene missed called her phone.

Chapter 22

"The night is under my control." Annika was in bed and it was only half past 8 in the evening, this was the first time Annika had decided to go to sleep really early. The reason being was because of Sheena's situation and the pressure of revision caused Annika to become separated from reality. Her brain was compact with notes and she felt fully prepared to take all her exams within one day, but she knew that wasn't possible. Because she was on study leave it meant that she could wake up late as there was no school to rush for. The only times she went to school was to take her exams and thereafter she could enjoy a 3 month long break before she started university.

The next morning Annika didn't get up until 10 o'clock, therefore she definitely had a long relaxing sleep. Most of the times when she got up in the morning her feelings were closely related to depression portraying a very bad mood, thus the only thing that would cheer her up was her breakfast, something she really admired. You couldn't blame the way she felt because not only she recently left her school, moreover at the same time her revision took most of the day and she had to pursue her daily household responsibilities. When she was at school all the tension at home was removed from her mind but now she had become even closer to them. Annika's revision tactics revealed useful methods to approach when coming to revise for any examination. If you had walked into Annika's bedroom during her revision period her wall was jam-packed with notes, they were neatly organised flourishing with vibrant highlighter marks. The majority of the wall was covered with notes for her English A level. This was because she had to memorise a huge amount of quotations and the only way through it was by sticking the quotes on the wall, this way she could notice them everyday so that they remained in her head.

Along with Annika's revision the sole worrying event that made Annika anxious nearly everyday was Tony coming to find out about Sheena who was not yet over Ashley. She prayed to her God that Tony didn't come to find out about Sheena during her exams or wished that he never came to know. She left the rest up to God.

"Monotonous May" Annika signed as her first exam was only a couple of days away, but she was 100% positive that she had revised accordingly and when it came to confronting her allocated examinations she will try her level best to gain her predicted grades. Throughout the month of May until the first week in June Annika undertook her exams courageously with great relief at the end of it.

Once her final examination concluded, Annika and all her friends decided to meet up at their favourite café. They met up to decide about their leaver's prom and whether everything was under control for the day. The leaver's prom was only two weeks away, at the table of the café where they sat, Annika and her friends over talked each other to make sure the arrangements were fully set for the day. Because all of their examinations were over they decided not to talk about them whilst they were having their hot beverages.

When Annika got home from the café she doubled checked her outfit was prepared for a spectacular night as the prom was only two weeks away. Her outfit was an Asian dress which was a soft lilac colour with silver embroidery. To complete the outfit she bought a dazzling silver handbag, glamorous pointed sandals and a lilac pendant set. She had promised her friends that she would transform for the day, regardless of whether Tony liked it or, she was determined to keep her friends promises as it wasn't ideal to break them when it was their last night together.

July 2004, this was when Annika started her first job which was at the restaurant. It took her two months straight to find her first job and the only way she did this was to remain self determined and whatever job came across she would take it. This was how she searched and finalised her first job at the restaurant. Rita had decided to go to India whilst Annika was on her summer break, therefore Annika had decided to terminate her employment because she was going for 4 weeks and when she came back from her holiday she had already confirmed to find a new job. Unfortunately when it came to Annika's last day at work, her manager reminded her throughout the day that there will always be a job for her if she ever needed it back. There was a sense of invisible sadness peaking from her work colleagues this was because Annika was admired truly by all her colleagues and they desperately didn't want her to leave.

As usual Annika's final words at work were "we all have to move on one day." She gathered to think about what the future held for her, due to the fact that most of the children in the Manda family were brought up in a less preferable manner. Annika, Sheena, Kareena and Adi consistently contemplated that even though they might have experienced a harrowing childhood God will still give them a blissful future. Generally,

Annika comprehended with her existence by allowing herself to appreciate and encounter life events correctly and if they are complex resolute them without failure. God will take this into account and consider luxurious prospects. The thought of looking forward to tomorrow made her ecstatic, thus you can only ever imagine the perfect perspective but, this was never true.

Chapter 23

The prom was only a week away now, therefore Annika begun to count the days. Despite this for a moment, Rita had arranged to go to India after the prom also she decided to book a week in Goa whilst they visited incredible India. Moreover, Sheena had decided to come along as well hence Tony eagerly booked the tickets, so this was going to be a definite summer Annika would never forget. Rita was full of thrill and Sheena was glad to get out of the house for a full month and from her job. As the days hurried by the Manda family started to get back to normal and Sheena's state of affairs was still buried under the ground however could have erupted anytime or any day if Tony came to know of Sheena's mischievous acts.

The prom landed on a Saturday and it was arranged to start after 6 o'clock in the evening. Because Annika was now free on Saturdays she could plan the rest of the day appropriately. Ever since she was young her life ruled around a set routine because she could assure herself that she was being efficient with time including an enhancement in her ability to use her own initiative. Annika prepared herself for the evening to come, she popped on her outfit and told Serene to come to her house to style her hair. Annika decided to spiral her hair and wear purple coloured contact lenses to integrate with her evening dress, Serene beautifully curled Annika's hair and helped with putting on a touch of make up. Serene wore a black evening dress, high heeled sandals complementing with sparkling silver jewellery. Once Annika was complete, when she walked down the stairs Tony was astonished to see Annika but he remained silent as Serene was present and walked into the lounge. Serene and Annika had to quickly rush to Rebecca's house whom only lived 5 minutes away because it was Rebecca's mum who was taking them to the hotel. Rita dropped of Serene and Annika to Rebecca's house, when they got there Rita told Annika not to be late otherwise Tony will fuse, Annika assured her mother that she would be home by 11 o'clock.

The prom was held at an established venue located in the middle of a tidy and eye catching rural area. Rebecca, Annika and Serene got to the hotel by half past 7 and everyone was gathered outside the hotel to meet and greet before they went inside. Annika felt very anxious because she thought she had overly dressed herself and there was never an occasion when Annika did dress up. Therefore, it was her opportunity to liberate and enjoy the evening without thinking about Tony's opinion about the way she looked and when she got home whether Tony would ask her 100 questions. The atmosphere at the prom was absolutely remarkable, because everyone enjoyed themselves and danced the whole night away. The teachers were having the time of their lives because they were separated from all the marking and teaching they had to do for the night. Annika for the first time remained very happy and experienced such a great night, that time flew by because she was having the best time of her life. It came to 11 o'clock in the evening Annika rang Rita to pick her up along with Serene and Rebecca. She was glad to have gone home with her two closest mates. After dropping off Serene and Rebecca home Annika was exhausted, when she got home she slept in her outfit and didn't wake up till late the next morning.

The next time Annika recalled the leaver's prom was on the aeroplane. It took between 8-10 hours to get to India from England. When Rita, Annika and Sheena got to India they all suffered from jet lag, so straightaway they slept for at least 6 hours without distraction.

The moments in India Annika cherished was the week they spent in Goa. The hotel they stayed at was next to a glamorous beach in which the sand consisted of numerous shady shells. Annika grabbed the opportunity to collect a hand full of her favourite looking shells whilst Sheena enjoyed sitting under the sun and watching beyond the sea. Rita walked around the beach wondering about back home, how Tony would be coping and that Adi didn't cause any uproar with him. Their accommodation in the hotel was the most cleanest and luxurious room they had ever relaxed in. They had booked the one room for all three of them and most importantly it came with a balcony where you could watch the beach and the sea sway with the weather. The night time was the best time to view the gorgeous scenery of the beach and swinging green palm trees not forgetting the startling sky incorporated with the shimmering stars. Sheena took pictures on the night and all the attractions they had visited before it came to an end. Due to all the fun that was generated in India for a month, time was uncontrollably hasty causing the departure from India to arrive in England for Rita, Annika and Sheena quickly. Annika had adjusted to the lifestyle in India perhaps wanting to permanently emigrate in the coming future.

Chapter 24

After the 4 weeks in indulging India, Annika was distraught to come to England's cold weather. She knew she had to look for a new job before she had started her university so that she wouldn't be sitting indolently for 2 months. Annika was the type of girl who had an intrinsic value of keeping busy therefore her second job had to be productive just like her previous job. She wanted to work near home so the best place to apply for a job was in the high street. Additionally, high streets were always looking for young part time individuals. Her sole aim was to find a job in a bank and all the commercial banks were located in the high street, but whenever she applied for a position at a bank they wanted people who would be available for full time and have previous experience in the area of customer services. Thereon, she searched for a job which involved the role

Behind Closed Doors

of approaching and meeting the needs of customers, after 2 weeks of hunting for employment she gradually gained a position in a selling phones. Subsequently undergoing the interview process Annika was content she would now gain the experience needed to work in a bank. As it took her just over a month to find a new job, she prepared herself to start university in just under 3 weeks; all the paperwork and modules for her course were up to grabs so that when she started her first day everything was under control even though her instincts told her something was bound to go wrong.

Before Annika started university she worked full time at her new job so that time passed quickly for her to commence her higher education. At the university there were many places to socialise in however, Annika wasn't thrilled by the sight of them, Annika's anti social traits kicked in but you couldn't blame the way she designed her life because she was nurtured within restrictions which caused her thinking to also change with her upbringing. Her maturation was exceptional therefore, it didn't mean she lacked to lead the enrichments of life it was her way of living.

The hot topic that rolled off Annika's tongue was her new employment. She always spoke about how wonderful her work colleagues were and how much they appreciated her personality within the company. Annika portrayed oneself to be quite introverted and shy, thus her skills in confidence and determination weren't yet let free, but she knew that it was this job that would have boosted her strength of mind. Before Annika started her job she was completely unaware of the mechanics of phones, after a month of being at her job her language vocabulary expanded to the new specifications of phones.

Most of Annika's friends decided to live away from home to go to university, many of them found places miles away from Wullington as it was a chance for them to experience their independency. As a whole the majority of them were spread across England however, Annika was content that Rebecca remained nearby as she was her childhood friend. Before all of her friends moved away from home Annika celebrated her birthday keeping in mind it was a good way of getting everyone together once they moved. Annika arranged her birthday to take place in a lavishing Italian restaurant which was complete with perfection in every corner and side. The restaurant was the most elegant venue to celebrate a perfectly loyal person's birthday which was born within Annika. Serene and Rebecca were the first people at the restaurant joined with many more friends, the whole of the restaurant was taken up by the majority of Annika's friends therefore from this point on Annika realised the utmost passion her friends had within her, a tear dropped from her left eye as she overlooked all her friends sitting around the spherical table arranged formally. A sense of nostalgia crossed Annika's mind when she watched all her friends cheer and tuck into their luscious meals. It was the reminder to her that this would have been the last time after a while they would see each other hence she had to make the most of it. During the day Annika was showered with a numerous amount of gifts which made her smile and cry at the same time as she couldn't refuse any of the gifts. The celebration of her birthday lasted throughout the day until it ended at 6 o' clock in the evening since Tony would have expected her back home as she was gone since 12 noon. The reason why she didn't go out in the night for her birthday was because Tony was the kind of father whom didn't let his children out to bars and clubs.

Fortunate for Annika she felt her new job was very productive and efficient to adjust to. Annika never had a problem to working in a very high motivational environment because it was a new skill added to her curriculum vitae and her personality which in effect enhanced her self confidence. Her constant perspective of the company was that it was thousand times better than her previous job, this was because she was paid really well, moreover Annika was the kind of girl who planned her future thus her current job provided her with the beneficial skills. Not only, she worked with the opposite gender as her previous job consisted of females this helped to support her social skills which weren't as strong as other girls she knew off. As a result the company gave her the chance to improve her communication and self-assurance skills in order to make use of them in the coming future. From very long time Annika didn't have admirable feelings for the opposite sex, however the tables turned because she worked with a sweet and benevolent guy that made her somewhat attracted to him perhaps this was a start to Annika's little imaginary world which becomes almost true when you understand it. Day by day working by him made her feelings grow for him. His name was Colin who was at least 5 years older than her however age was not a concern it was the personality and the person within him. Was this a new journey for Annika?

On the contrary, at university her new friends were very considerate and supportive, Annika never doubted their friendship with her thereby her trust within them was a valuable matter to her. Importantly she made new friends at a minimum level at university this was because from her high school she had an endless list of friends which made it harder for her to move on therefore, making a lot of new friends was twice the amount of effort also when coming to leave university after 3 years.

Chapter 25

In the most sweet but short epilogue, Colin from day one blinded Annika with his everlasting compassionate charms. Colin didn't have the slightest notion that Annika adored him, yet Annika wanted Colin's lack of awareness to stay this way. From the past, Annika's affection towards guys were unrequited therefore her discernment saw a pattern emerge; in this case she was 100% sure her attraction to Colin would be unrequited just like the other past affairs. For Annika it was another entity altogether in which only Colin existed, her preoccupied moments kept her awake nearly every night and before going to bed she would switch the light off, stand by her window and look out into the midnight blue sky. Frequently every night Annika imagined she had control over the night and it was at these moments where she stood by her window and experienced an odd sensation wanting to be very close with Colin. She knew that she couldn't indulge in such temptations since the reality was much different. Despondently Annika would say every night,

"Goodnight Colin I hope all your dreams and wishes come true" directly inspecting the moon.

Furthermore, because Annika couldn't cross her boundaries and she could never pursue her desires, thus she created her own imaginary lifestyle of being with Colin, these kept her hopeful perhaps one day she could experience being his girlfriend and if this was the case she would only allow this for a short period of time. At work Colin was generous but quite strict in general but Annika didn't take it personally when he became stern towards her. Annika at times didn't mind his attitude because she lived under strict conditions at home and it didn't bother her if she did at work. Annika theorised Colin's attitude to be stringent and precocious because he aspired to portray to his boss that he would be capable of running his own store in the future.

Annika's prudence noted every single instant she came in contact with Colin; the pettiest little moments were of great prominence to her. There were times where she had bad incidents with him however her explanation to this would have been Colin doing his job correctly, the moments were also attached with pleasant times allowing for these to become etched memories. It was instances like these causing Annika's attachment to develop further more towards Colin. Altogether Colin was the complete opposite to Annika but it was common sense that "opposites attract", in Annika's situation this wasn't proven. The affection could be described near enough to an obsession or Annika's expression of "a beautiful mind complementing a sheer striver." There was nothing which precluded Annika from disliking Colin and from there on she continued to like him. Nothing or nobody interfered with her new world.

It only came to a crunch when he left from Wullington to another store after 2 months, Annika was absolutely disheartened whom in her own time cried in pain. The day he left from work was her day off from work; with great self-belief she gave him white roses to depict her friendship towards him. Psychologically, her main reason that stopped Annika from undermining her requests internally was because she felt that she didn't have the beauty to win any guy or even Colin. Therefore, Annika's interpretation of her personality was akin to naivety and precautious and her only escape from reality was her own imagination.

Chapter 26

"Oh well, so what if I can't get what I want, there is no harm in dreaming for my temptations" Annika remarked to her God. The only person Annika could talk to about her inner most deep feelings was to her God. She would happily explain to her God how the day went at work now that Colin wasn't working there anymore. Because she worked in sales there was always a minimum target to he hit hence, it meant Annika working till the evening. This made Tony doubtful and he would comment to Rita saying "these things are going to cause Annika to go astray, because she stays quite late at work we don't know what she gets up to" accidentally Annika over heard her parent's remarks regarding her job. "Why can't I get my own freedom, a job is a job, now they are going to think inadequately of me" she commented to herself in return. Rita couldn't say anything in return to Tony's comment because she knew he would explode at her if she went against him.

Most of the evenings were normal at the Manda's house however when it came to cooking the dinner in the evening, Annika would be reduced to doing it herself. Kareena would purposely not help her because she wanted to know whether Sheena's situation was over yet. One evening in the kitchen Kareena kept pestering her to confess whether she knew what Sheena was up to? Unexpectedly Annika shouted "why don't you leave me alone and shurrup? Go and ask Sheena yourself I don't know anything"

"I know you know something, you're like her shadow in disguise that always follows her,"

"bloody heck, I don't know anything" Annika ended.

"ANNIKA" Tony yelled from inside the lounge. She opens the door and walks into the lounge, he continued to remark

"nowadays you are becoming very bigheaded and you are starting to talk back, don't speak to your elder sister in such a manner. We know you learn it off Sheena"

"Oh my God what have I done now" Sheena mumbles rolling her eyes. Annika's face saddened and since the past months all Tony has ever moaned about is his own worries and Annika becoming disrespectable.

"You always say this to me, I am not like Sheena, and it's not fair" She bursts into tears and runs across the lounge upstairs to her bedroom. Annika's eye's poured with water and ruined her fair skinned face. She starts whooping and wipes her face with her sleeve, sitting on her bed with the light switched off facing directly outside with her curtains wide open. She continuously kept crying that night and mournfully said

"Only if I could go from here, no one cares or loves me in this family. Why am I compared to Sheena when I do nothing that is similar to her? It just not fair, I cook, clean, and sensibly do my university work. I never go out and have been working since I was 16 years old, so I can secure my future, please show me a way out God."

After a few moments later, Tony called Annika to come downstairs to wash up the dishes. Annika had no choice but to go otherwise Tony would be 100% assured that Annika was becoming corrupted. Following the washing up Annika decided to go to bed but Tony stopped her.

"Stay down here, we want to talk to you" Tony obnoxiously said. Annika nodded her head side to side standing by the door.

"What was that for? Sit here and can you explain to me why you have such an attitude on you? And when you speak to us you speak in an impudent approach. Is it because you are getting older and you believe you can talk back to your parents? Always remember that I don't like back chatters and in this house whatever I say goes." Tony explained to Annika.

"There's' nothing wrong with me, why do you have to ask so many questions like I am a feisty child? Can't you see I am the only responsible one here and the rest of them are dependant on you?"

"What, so aren't you dependant on us anymore? You have grown up so fast now have you?"

"I don't mean it like that dad. You can't hold our hands forever; you have to let go of our hands one day. Look at Kareena she is the oldest in the family but yet you control where she can work" Annika gasped.

"Well, well Rita look who it is, miss know it all. Is it your university work that is getting to your head?" Tony replied in great anger

Annika stutters and gets up to leave the lounge but Tony was adamant for her to stay and give her explanation.

"Don't go barging off, finish off what you have to say"

"I have nothing left to say, you are always going to be controlling and patriarchal. Why can't you ever listen to our feelings and happiness then maybe you will understand why your children are so repellent of you."

Tony starts to boil with hostility; it is obvious that the truth is too bitter for him and the fact that it was coming from his daughter. This was even more harrowing because the last time someone spoke against

Tony it wasn't too good at the end of it. But would Tony hurt Annika?

"Annika I suggest you should start putting you act together because it's not going to be nice what I could say?" Tony becomes even more petulant and bangs the table with his hand in front of him.

"Why you going to hurt me like you always have?" Annika furiously said. Tony looks at Annika in great despair, his eyes are near enough about to pop out and states "Why don't you go back where you came from? Rita we have committed the biggest mistake of adopting Annika from your friend, we should have put her in an orphanage."

Everyone turns their face and are emotionally gob smacked to Tony's comment especially nnika.

Chapter 27

The Manda family weren't perfect after all. Tony and Rita spoke about their family to others like they were a pot of gold and that their children were courageous and doing well in their studies. Every time Tony and Rita visited relatives they would enhance their family image especially Tony who triggered it off

"Oh my daughter and son are doing exceptionally well in their studies that they will be applying for high income jobs". The funny thing was Tony didn't even know what their children were studying so how would he have known if they were doing exceptionally good. It was more likely Annika who did positively great in her studies but Tony and Rita were unaware of this. Tony would deceivingly say "we allow our children to go out wherever they want otherwise they start to moan if I don't let them go out, however they do make sure that they don't drink alcohol. I have drilled into my kids enjoy life but don't commit mistakes that you will regret later on in life." This was what made people outside look upon the Manda family for inspiration but behind close doors it was absolutely berserk, it was a mad and maniac house which repeatedly caused arguments every day.

Contemporarily behind close doors everybody is different, even when they face the reality individuals will put on a superficial front to build an idyllic view to others. This wasn't just in Asian cultures it was apparent in every culture, it was harmless to boost your family image just to remain within society's needs. Furthermore, because it became a common movement it could have been interpreted as an innate social norm passing onto generations. In addition this preconception of having a perfect family was distinguished many years ago during our ancestors, but there was no harm in trying to be immaculate for your own purposes.

Why was it families wanted to maintain such images? There was no reward as today everyone did for themselves. One of the philosophy born from this was that your own became strangers and strangers became your own, perhaps it was an indication to the current generation accepting their close friends to be valuable people in their lives, whereas families were becoming second best. This could lead to a potential problem because later on in life it is your family that you will need for support not your friends since they might need to support their own families. Also as you encounter life, one day you have to move on and just like Annika and her friends they all decided to go separate directions to reach their own destinations. Besides it wasn't wrong to make friends, it was right to have friends because it meant you could tell them secrets in which you couldn't tell your parents therefore they would be important as guidance in helpless situations.

Chapter 28

"What do you mean adopted dad?" Adi said curiously, Tony's face was ferocious and deep red because he had let out the deepest and darkest secret in the family. There was silence for a few moments, and Rita had broke the silence after a few minutes

"Surely, you heard wrong Adi?"

"No he said we have made the biggest mistake in adopting Annika from your friend" he looks at Tony and says

"Dad"

Tony turns around to Rita "well, she has to find out one day, she believes she is old enough to talk back to us nowadays, so what's the problem?"

Tony then faces Annika who gasps at the look on her face then taking a deep breath and swallowing his saliva Tony commences by

"The truth is Annika, you aren't our real daughter, we adopted you when you were about 3 years old, and it is a very long story. You were your mum's best mate's daughter who isn't in this world anymore. She was suffering from cancer and was at her last stage, her husband had died in a car accident because he was intoxicated by alcohol. Therefore, when Pam found out she was diagnosed with cancer it was too late to cure it and you were only little so she decided to give you to us."

The shock of Annika's life clandestine was revealed, her expression was complete bewilderment and speechless. Adi couldn't believe a single word Tony had just said and knowing Annika was not his real sister pinched him right by the heart. Sheena and Kareena already knew about Annika being adopted as they were around 10 years old when Annika came into their house. For the past 16 years the Manda family kept Annika in the dark thinking that she was part of the family but in reality she was a lonely child who was living with complete strangers.

"How come I didn't know this in the first place? Why couldn't you tell me and Annika before?" Adi interrupts

"It doesn't make a difference Annika is still our child" Rita speaks out.

Annika bursts out crying and gets up to leave the room before she goes she states sadly "Well, it does make a difference to me RITA! No wonder you all treat me separate from the family and always make comments about me like I am invisible"

"get back here, because you have found out the truth it doesn't mean you stop acting like you aren't part of the family, just calm down and let the night pass like nothing ever happened." Tony expresses.

"You lot can act like nothing has happened but it is vital to me, now I know why I was isolated in this family and felt like I didn't belong here. Why couldn't you make me feel like I was wanted I done everything for this family and house I even took care of granddad who isn't even my granddad. It is true strangers do become part of a family and respect's those in the family without question and you lot who are his real grandchildren couldn't even take care of him. I am ashamed." Annika thunders out of the lounge and slams the door behind her. The rest of the family silently sit in the lounge and there is some muttering going on between Adi, Kareena and Sheena.

"You didn't need to tell her that she was adopted Tony, now she is going to really hate us. I don't understand why she said we have made her feel unwanted in this family, when I nurtured her like my own" Rita mentions to Tony.

"That's only because she is angry, don't worry she will get over it. It's probably all the university work as well getting to her head and she believes she has grown up now, she can't say or do things her way otherwise she will turn out to be like Sheena, I bet it's Sheena who has influenced her to act in such an inappropriate way."

"As you say that dad she is sensible enough not be influenced by me, just face it dad you have caused Annika to think in this way" Sheena raucously says.

Rita goes into the kitchen and stands by the cooker; it seems like Rita is hiding something, she beings to hold on to her stomach and mumbles to herself a few words akin to "what's going to happen if he finds out the real truth?"

Chapter 29

A couple of hours speed on by, everyone is fast asleep, and it is only Annika who is wide awake in the silent night in her room. The light was switched off as usual in Annika's room and Annika was sitting on her black wheelie chair placed next to her bed. She never feared the dark or night because it was the only time she felt she was in control of the day. The only light in her room came from the dimmed lamp which didn't make much of a difference. Her face was dried with tears and you could notice the white smudgy marks stained on her glasses from all the crying. It was approximately 1.50am in the morning and Annika remained awake. It was obvious it was going to be very difficult for Annika now on as she had only found out a few hours ago that Rita and Tony weren't her real parents. After sitting in the dark for 3 hours she thought hard and straight and the look on her face made you wonder twice to what Annika had spinning in her highly knowledgeable head, there was a sense of eeriness about to emerge as she constantly glanced at her watch. It took her half an hour to think, when suddenly she got up and pulled down her suitcase, once the suitcase was in front of her she opened it and whiffed the odd smell that developed from it and without a second thought she continued to throw in her essentials and clothes. Moreover she took out her smaller bags and filled them with her remaining clothes so that she knew she wouldn't have to come back for anything when she had gone. The seconds ticked away on the clock motivating her to hasten up and keeping her final decision intact. Meanwhile, she took out her bank books, passport and other important documents to take with her for unexpected events.

Next to her was a notepad, she ripped a sheet of paper out of it and wrote a note with a black biro

<u>Dear Mum and Dad</u>

I never doubted your upbringing and I won't blame you for the reason why I left this house so dad that's one less responsibility for you now. I think you lot will be better of without me and since I am 19 years old, I feel as if I am old enough to leave and it's over the legal age for me to leave. I will always cherish your love and care you gave me since I have been a child and I really appreciate both of your nurturing towards me and accepting someone else's child like your own. Sheena, Adi and Kareena have always been part of my heart and they will always be, I never doubted our relationship and I still today accept them as my brother and sisters even though I'm not their baby sister anymore. Dad, please forgive Sheena because I know deep down inside you haven't forgiven her yet, it would be for the best and then you will find out what she really wants.

Don't worry dad I have learnt how to look after myself as you have never let me go out and staying stuck at home has given me my own sense of independency. Now that I am not there you have to have complete trust in me in ruling my own life and don't worry I will pursue all your traditions and live within the restriction you gave me here. Dad, I have become used to living under your boundaries and if I dare cross them I know it would be wrong. Perhaps, one day I will come back, if not just accept me like I was another daughter you never had. I am really sorry and I hope you can forgive me.

P.S make sure granddad has his tablets on time and I know he will ask questions but it's up to you to tell him the truth.

LUV YOU ALL SO MUCH
<u>*ANNI*</u>
XxX

Subsequently Annika started to cry uncontrollably and when she was really upset the thought of Colin crossed her mind keeping her content, she then decided to write a note to Colin and send it to his current workplace.

<u>*To Colin*</u>

I know this maybe strange but what I am going to write in this letter is my inner feelings for you. When you first came to Wullington store to work, you stole my heart away and my heart had decided to accept your attraction. Up until this present day I remain very affectionate towards you. However, I know that you can't like me in return and I have never questioned your belief and I will not. Because of this I have come to a decision that I will let my feelings for you fade away. I know they say absence makes the heart grow fonder but this only applies to couples in love with each other. You probably will never hear from me again after this letter. Unfortunately it is for the best otherwise I will keep deceiving myself. Finally I would like to say, Colin you were the most honest, shrewd and amazing person I have ever met in my entire life your character is very inspirational that made me learn certain things in life in which I will never forget. I wish the best of luck for your future and my blessings will always be with you until the day I die. Take care of yourself.

Love you loads
<u>*Annika*</u>
XxX

Once she had finished writing the letters hoping her parents and Colin will understand her feelings she neatly folded them both and popped both of the letters in separate envelopes. Thereafter Annika slept for 2 hours and it wasn't until 5'o clock in the morning when she woke up. Quietly Annika wiped her face with a wet towel and contacted a taxi in which she remembered the phone number off the top of her head. She told the taxi driver on the phone to come and collect her from her house in 10 minutes, making him aware not to beep the horn when he came. Before the taxi arrived Annika entered her parent's room calmly and looked at them both, a tear rolled down her face following a number of tears and before she made a noise and became uncontrollably upset she quickly left the house leaving her house keys on the note she left for her parents. Outside the Manda house the taxi driver had arrived and when he came Annika picked up her luggage and placed them in the boot of the taxi she then told the driver to take her to the train station. Annika was now long gone from the Manda family.

Chapter 30

Later on in the same day, once Tony and Rita woke up from bed they didn't even bother to check to see if Annika was all right after yesterday's performance. It was not until Rita made breakfast for Tony she realised to wake Annika up. Once she gave Tony his breakfast she came running upstairs to Annika's bedroom, when she entered her room her face froze when she noticed a note with keys on top of Annika's comfy double bed. Fearfully walking towards the bed she picked up the letter and began to read it. Rita collapsed on to Annika's bed and she became very upset with tears pouring down her face. Rita got up and went running down the stairs to the lounge to show Tony the consequences of his mistake.

"Look what you have done now" Rita shouted at Tony

Rita passed the letter to Tony and in the kitchen Adi, Sheena and Kareena watched uninformed. After reading the note, Tony couldn't believe his eyes and thought he was dreaming that he begun to slap himself.

"What does she mean by forgiving Sheena and then I would know what Sheena really wants?" Tony looks at Sheena whom is standing in disbelief he then tells her to come into the lounge.

"Well, Sheena what have you got to say about this?"

"Annika's probably just being her good old self; you know how much she wanted you to forgive me so that we all could get on"

"Nah there is more to it than that, otherwise she would have not wrote what you really want. Sheena you got to tell me now, otherwise I will find out one day" he continued to say.

Sheena looks at her mum who doesn't give her any sign of help.

"Okay dad I'll tell you the truth, but you have to promise me that you won't hit the roof"

"I hope it isn't what I think it is?" he replies back to Sheena

Sheena takes a deep breath and tells her dad the real truth

"Dad I was never over Ashley I still like him today and I still see him……. I can't help myself…….. I just want to be with him otherwise I will never be happy and this family will never reunite how it used to be"

"you stupid idiot, all along you was taking me for a ride. I can never forgive you for what you have done especially facing me everyday knowing you were in the wrong. Just get out of my face before I do something stupid." Sheena knew she had to go from there therefore Adi and Kareena went with Sheena to search for Annika.

In the mean time Rita knew this was all down to Tony and she couldn't sit any longer without telling him the real truth.

"This is your entire fault Tony, if only you understood her feelings and wants or kept your big mouth shut we wouldn't have to see this day" Rita came out with

"well, she would have found out one day and then would she have left?"

"Sometimes you can be so obnoxious Tony, why could not you have listened to your children and gave them what they wanted. You always kept them behind close door especially Annika. This is why she became defiant and detached from you. Knock, knock Tony we are living in the 21st century."

Tony knew Rita was right he sat with his head in his hands holding his hair tightly whilst Rita kept moving back and forth like a pendulum on a clock. Rita went up to Tony and sat next to him on the sofa, she told Tony to face her,

"Tony, I should have told you the truth years back and I no it is too late to say, how am I……. going to say this to you……um…. Annika is our real daughter she wasn't Pam's daughter" Rita expressed.

In great disbelief Tony was near enough about to slap Rita but he stopped

"WHAT! How is this possible?"

"When you went to America I found out I was pregnant and after losing the business I knew we weren't financially fit to bring up another child, but I was helpless and I couldn't abort the baby. Therefore, if I had told you the truth in the first place I knew you wouldn't want this baby because of the money. So whilst you were in America for 3 years I planned to keep the child and the girls had promised me not to tell you about this until the time was right."

"Ohhhhhh my God…. Rita what have you done?" Tony rages in fury and

he gets up and slaps Rita across the face without Rita's alertness he then looks directly at the wall in front of him and mutters to Rita

"We have lost Annika forever; she is probably miles away now."

Rita is stunned by Tony's behaviour; she knew he was experiencing a sense of remorse and if he had control of time he would have changed everything to stop Annika from leaving.

"Are you happy now after slapping me? It won't make a difference and what I did was for the best, if I had told you, you would have told me to abort Annika and then you wouldn't have had such a respectable daughter. Annika was the heart of this family and she kept us all worthy of remaining as a family but you had to drive her away. If only it hadn't been for your controlling and dogmatic behaviour none of our children would be so scared of you."

For once this time it was Rita that had to control the decisions for the family and not Tony. Perhaps it was meant to be Rita that a long time ago was to change Tony's stubborn personality but would he have listened to her?

"Your right Rita, I have to change otherwise I will lose all of my children, only if Annika came back so that she knew I was a changed man and she knew my inner feelings. She was my only favourite daughter because she kept this family intact for us." It was unbelievably true Tony had realised he had been so obstinate and the outcome of the current situation would only have a solution by his change in behaviour. Moreover, this change would have to be permanent because this was the only way his family would remain united. Now Annika was gone it was too late for Tony to change his character because the rest of the family would never forgive Tony for what he did and it wouldn't bring Annika back home.

Tony and Rita sat on the sofa holding each other's hands and praying that Annika would come back home, all they had left now was hope.

Will Annika come to know that Tony and Rita are her real parents after all?

THE END

Amita Tak is a student studying an undergraduate combined honours degree and works part time in sales. Her ambition since she was young was to write a book and today Behind Close Doors has fulfilled this dream. She lives in Wolverhampton with her loving family. Do deeply appreciate her exclusive novel in which she hopes her audience are enthralled by.

About the Author

Amita Tak is a student studying an undergraduate combined honours degree. Her ambition since she was young was to write a book and today behind close doors has fulfilled her dream. Amita's sole aim was to pursue the dream of publishing a book in which she hopes to inflence many potential young writers. She loves to dance to maintain her health and help those in need. At the moment she is studying a degree in Accounting and Psychology in order to develop her future career in finance. Whereas Psychology is her second area of interest and support for future requirements if confronted. Lastly, Amita has been nurtured to cook great indian food leaving everyone indulged and without any loss of appetite.

Printed in Great
Britain
by Amazon